D0181350

BLACK SPIDER
OVER
TIEGENHOF

Other novels by James D. Yoder

The Yoder Outsiders
Sarah of the Border Wars
Barbara: Sarah's Legacy

BLACK SPIDER OVER TIEGENHOF

JAMES D. YODER

HERALD PRESS
Scottdale, Pennsylvania
Waterloo, Ontario

Library of Congress Cataloging-in-Publication Data
Yoder, James D., 1929-
  Black spider over Tiegenhof / James D. Yoder
    p. cm.
  ISBN 0-8361-9012-2
  1. World War, 1939-1945—Germany—Fiction. 2. Mennonites—
Germany—History—20th century—Fiction. 3. Holocaust, Jewish
(1939-1945)—Fiction. I. Title.
PS3575. 028B53
813′ .54—dc20

94-39150
CIP

The paper used in this publication is recycled and meets the minimum
requirements of American National Standard for Information Sciences
—Permanence of Paper for Printed Library Materials, ANSI Z39.48-
1984.

Scripture quotations are from the King James Version of the Bible.

BLACK SPIDER OVER TIEGENHOF is a work of fiction. Though the
author did considerable research regarding background, setting, and
Mennonite culture of the Werder during the period involved, all
characters are fictional. Any resemblance to persons presently living
would be only coincidental.

BLACK SPIDER OVER TIEGENHOF
Copyright © 1995 by Herald Press, Scottdale, Pa. 15683
      Published simultaneously in Canada by Herald Press,
      Waterloo, Ont. N2L 6H7. All rights reserved
Library of Congress Catalog Number: 94-39150
International Standard Book Number: 0-8361-9012-2
Printed in the United States of America
Book and cover design by Merrill R. Miller

00 99 98 97 96 95 10 9 8 7 6 5 4 3 2 1

To Ernst Penner,
whose life of courage and faith inspired this novel

Acknowledgments

Though I am indebted to many persons who shared episodes and stories from personal accounts of their experiences in the Nazi era, I especially remember the following persons for enabling me to establish the outline and background for this story: Ernst Penner, Newton, Kansas; Henry and Beatrice Rosenthal Buller, Beaumont, Texas; Winfield Fretz, North Newton, Kansas; Henry Claassen, North Newton, Kansas; Erwin Goering, Moundridge, Kansas; Lottie Penner, Newton, Kansas; Dr. Milton Claassen, Newton, Kansas; and Ethel Abrahams, North Newton, Kansas. In addition, I am indebted to John Thiesen, archivist, and his staff at the Mennonite Library and Archives, North Newton, Kansas, for their assistance in helping me with the background research.

BLACK SPIDER
OVER
TIEGENHOF

1

It wasn't until Esther Claassen had shut her iron oven door that she realized her left hand was clutching her throat. Hermann's words drifting in from the blue room brought on the old fear—of a mother losing her son.

"From the Advanced Hitler Youth, Uncle Peter, I enter the Führer's Reichswehr (the leader's defense force). I can hardly wait to join the batallion, boots, uniform, all for the 'glory of the Führer."

A tragic memory of three years ago rose along with the heavy lump in her throat.

"Where's Hansa?" his twin brother, Christian, had called. "You'll find him. He is never far away." Actually, it was rare for the twins to be separated. Just where was Hansa? That cold April day seemed as yesterday.

They'd searched under the front porch. Hermann, the longest-legged, ran down the pasture toward the clover field. Christian tunneled through the hayloft. Still Hansa hadn't been found.

Esther concluded he was playing one of his tricks and would soon burst from under a raspberry bower.

Then the old hired man, Otto, said, "Maybe we'd better check the pond."

A grip frigid as a Siberian wind clutched Esther's heart. The pond was deep, purple, colder than the North Sea.

"He knows well enough to stay away from the pond, especially on a cold day like this." Gerhard assured her the boy couldn't possibly be near the pond.

Neither of the twins yet knew how to swim. Old Otto warned them almost daily how icy the water was.

Nevertheless, something drew her to the pond. At first she was unable to call out, terror-stricken at the sight of the small toy boat Grandfather Froese had whittled for him that very afternoon.

The grappling hooks clutched at her heart now. Gerhard and Otto had worked a full hour using those iron fingers to bring up her yellow-haired lad.

Now, Esther Claassen's heart again chilled, as words of eighteen-year-old Hermann drifted through the kitchen doorway. "The Führer, Herr Hitler, is our savior."

The words echoed from the blue room with the windows framing the green north German countryside. Uncle Peter, Gerhard, and her two sons leaned forward, engrossed in discussion.

Heat radiated from the iron stove and oven, warming the kitchen. Esther's eyes caught the few gathering clouds darkening in the east. "Another April shower," she whispered to herself, checking her apple cake again. Sudden thunder shook the windowpanes. Without thinking, she reached for a stewpot on the counter. Feeling the weight of it in her hand, she smiled to herself, realizing that when she was anxious she generally searched for her rolling pin or a stewpot.

"How did it get this way?" Esther murmured the words, not noticing that Chris, now eleven, had wandered into the kitchen. By "this way," Esther meant life under the Third Reich (empire) of the Führer—the control of it, the military marching of it, the hysterical unison of the choruses such as "Deutschland, erwache" (Germany, awake).

It seemed to Esther Claassen that the "Black Spider" held everything in its clutches.

"I can help you, Mother, since Violet isn't here anymore. I'll serve the cake and cold milk to Uncle Peter and the others."

That was like young Christian; he liked to help. Liked to risk and search out new corners of things, too. Like this Hitler Youth program and where it was leading. But all bright youngsters have inquisitive sides, don't they? She pondered it, wondering if she should caution him more.

Stepping across the gleaming tile floor, past the two great iron kettles low over their fireboxes, she put her arm around her blond son. He smelled like the new clover where he and Bruno had been rolling and playing.

Brushing back his cowlick, she smiled, a smile that covered the fear Hermann's words had caused. The warmth of his body against her side as she drew him close for a moment anchored her; the warmth glowed like the piece of amber on her bureau upstairs.

"Go sit with your father and Uncle Peter, Chris. Uncle Peter leaves for Kansas next Thursday. We may not see him again for—" Esther did not finish the sentence; the lad caught the fade-out of her voice and could sense the apprehension of his mother's heart.

So many changes for his parents, and for Hermann too. They noticed the changes more than he, as he had been too young to remember the bad times, the starving people, the hordes of unemployed. A "depression," they had called it.

He was too young to remember how it was when father came home from the Great War and their Fatherland was in defeat. Too young to remember the glorious day the Führer took office, voted in by the people.

Each day Chris and his classmates at school said, "Heil

(hail) Hitler," up to fifty times a day. He knew the meaning of the salute and the undulating black spider—the *swastika*—on the flag. A new cross, a new saving power for the Fatherland.

They all still laughed uproariously at the west bedroom upstairs, papered with thousand dollar deutsche marks. His father, Gerhard, worn and tired, had returned from Tiegenhof where he marketed the eggs and cream. He carried a loaf of bread in his hand and a basket overflowing with deutsche marks. "Not worth papering the wall with," Gerhard muttered.

Hermann, only seven, looked at the crisp, bright deutsche marks. "Since Father thinks they're worthless, I'll paper my bedroom wall with them."

That's what he had done. They chuckled to this day about it. They even took guests upstairs to have a look at the fabulous wall, now grown famous in their house.

Those times were past now. Almost every living room library table had a well-bound copy of Herr Hitler's *Mein Kampf* (My battle). The Führer was winning the battle for prosperity. Unemployment was at an end, even if folks were working in munitions plants. It was only for peace. Their own ministers clarified that for them: "Remember Romans 13; obey those who rule over you."

Esther seated herself in the kitchen rocker to watch the cake in the oven and the clustering clouds outside her window. Young Chris returned to the blue room, pulling a straight-backed chair near his father. His blue eyes focused on his brother Hermann. Could he ever be like him?

"Tell Uncle Peter about the swastika, Chris. You've been in the *Jungvolk* (Hitler youth guard) for a year. Already you're a brave little Reich soldier."

Nudged by Hermann, Chris began. "Well, Uncle Peter, since you immigrated to America when the times were hard, I guess you wouldn't know. Schoolmaster Schneider outlined it well. This was my oath: 'In the presence of this blood banner, which represents our Führer, I swear to devote all my energies and my strength to the savior of our country, Adolf Hitler. I am willing and ready to give up my life for him, so help me God.' "

Gerhard tapped the bowl of his pipe on his shoe heel and slipped it into his pocket, admiring the growing boy. A better world awaited Chris. The Führer promised.

"When we first put them up in school, the flags with the swastikas, I ran home. I was just a little boy, six years old. We had practiced saluting until my arm nearly fell off."

Esther lifted her hand to brush back a wisp of hair. Her shoulders tightened as she listened to her son. He had been so little, so innocent.

"Mother, Mother," he'd said. "There's a big black spider flying over Tiegenhof, the school, the City Hall, everywhere."

That's what he'd called it. The black spider. Most of the people thought it was an unsurpassed cross, announcing "Deutschland forever." But Esther remembered other days, other teachings, the soul-healing words from the New Testament: "Love your enemies; do good to those who hate you."

Rain began to pelt the red tile roof. Thunder jarred.

"The red background of the flag, said Herr Schneider, stands for all of us in a common cause, uniting the German workers, like the communists are together in their cause."

Hermann cleared his throat, looking straight at his younger brother. He didn't like that word "communist" and was glad the Führer's ideas advanced beyond communism. It was clear to all what was happening in Russia to the north.

"We use the word 'socialist,' " said Chris. "The white circle on the red field sets off the black swastika, a new cross. Not like the old cross of the churches.

"Herr Bowman, leader of our Hitler Youth, teaches that the old cross is outdated and stands for submission and weakness."

Uncle Peter, fifty-three and pompous in his serge suit, lifted his eyebrows at the proclamations of his nephews. He made feeble efforts to try not to appear better than the rest of his relatives, now that he was an American citizen.

"The swastika on the flag announces the Führer as Germany's savior and Germany forever." Christian's inquisitive nature leaped toward commitment when it came to the swastika, the new order, the Hitler Youth. His eyes gleamed.

"Correct," said Hermann, the freshly ironed shirt of his Hitler Jugend uniform setting off his dark hair.

"Haven't you read Herr Alfred Rosenberg's books, Uncle Peter? They describe the new religion that goes beyond the outdated views of the Jews in the Old Testament. I guess you could say the German flag announces the thousand-year reign of the glorious Aryan people. We are Aryan, Uncle Peter."

Drawing the fragrant apple cake from the oven, Esther placed it on the rack to cool. She'd serve it warm with the cold milk, allowing Chris to help her. Her hired girl, Violet, had left last month. The Fatherland required many industrious hands and Violet's brother had gone to serve in the Führer's army. Violet's mother, Marie Unruh, needed her.

Next week Esther planned to interview that heavyset new girl in Tiegenhof, Olga Fritzenheimer. There was more work on this farm than she could do by herself. Seeing the stewpot still on the counter, she grabbed the black handle and hung it above the chopping block. Nervous. The talk in the blue room was making her nervous.

"No doubt about it. People who visit Germany from

America say it is a miracle. The prosperity, the working to-gether, the feeling in the air. Whatever Hitler has done, most people think it is good. Still," said Uncle Peter, "I'm glad I left in '33." He cleared his throat, eyes focusing on the bound *Mein Kampf*.

Again he took out his gold turnip of a watch to check the time. He had not mentioned that he too—when he left to settle on the farms of Mennonite relatives in Kansas who had emigrated long before—had known the fear.

Uncle Peter didn't mention that in the year he left Ger-many all political parties except Nazi were outlawed. He didn't mention that Herr Goebbels took over the newspa-pers and the radio waves in the land. He didn't mention that to be Jewish was to lose your citizenship with all its rights. Uncle Peter was German himself, and from what he had picked up on this visit back to the old Mennonite com-munities of the Vistula area, it was best in this land not to criticize. Listen. Listen and ponder. Oh, share a little of how life is on the farm in Kansas, the church there. But say little about Hitler's Fatherland, or he might not get back to America.

Uncle Peter hoped his opulent belly didn't indicate sloth. He pulled his lapels and cleared his throat as he said, "In America, Hermann, Quakers, and Mennonites may choose alternative service to military service. They help in forestry, conservation work, and hospitals."

A silence hung for a while. Esther, leaning in the door frame, looked at him. She didn't have to be told that this was a dangerous topic for discussion. She knew Herr Hit-ler's Nazi leaders grouped conscientious objectors along with seditious people, outlaws, Gypsies, and Jews. She knew something about such uncooperative people being taken into "protective custody," whatever that was. But caution was best; one never knew who was listening.

Last evening at the supper table, Uncle Peter had put

down his glass of wine and chortled, "In the new Germany, I've noticed that everyone has taken on the German look." Then he laughed.

When they asked him to explain, he said, "Why, the German look is that quick turn of the head as everyone here looks over his shoulder."

That had shaken them. There was silence for a while, but the supper resumed as Esther passed the *plümemooss* (fruit soup).

A sadness touched her mouth. "Once our young men were exempt from military service. That was long ago. I remember when Pastor Schmidt and his little flock left for Russia, where they could hold their pacifist teachings, and Uncle Herbert and a few of our church members moved to Canada for the same reason. How did such precious parts of our faith fall by the wayside?" Esther realized that she probably shouldn't have said it, especially in front of Hermann. His commitment shone from his bright eyes. She, however, wondered to herself, *Is it possible to turn back?*

"You'll be going into the military next, won't you, Hermann?" Uncle Peter spoke to the intelligent, square-shouldered young man with the shining boots. Already his legs were trained in the disciplined marches, and his voice groomed for the phrases of joy and victory, *"Deutschland über alles"* (Germany overall).

His eyes gleamed with fervor and excitement for the Fatherland. "Mother, next week our Führer invites all advanced youth of the Jugend to the grand marches in Nürnberg (Nuremberg)."

2

Olga Fritzenheimer didn't like it that she was only five feet, five inches tall. Her many hearty appetites kept not only a thick rim of flesh around her middle, but also a burning lust for the things of the Führer.

However, she had long ago made peace with her body. What counted was what was inside a person. Even more, she had studied her *Rassenkunde* (racial science) to which she fully subscribed. Jews weren't German, their features showed that clearly. Herr Hitler was right on that one.

Over her wide head hung her yellow hair, cut in the style of the new German woman. A short bob, it was called. Actually, the cut was designed for a petite girl of Vienna or Berlin culture. Though it softened the front of her face, it clung in the back like the edge of a mixing bowl. Olga's head swayed with her square shoulders, as she cracked the whip over the rump of the horse straining to pull the buggy she'd rented.

"Get up, you black nag!" she cried. Olga chuckled to herself. No. She was not a bit threatened to have her interview with Frau Esther Claassen out past Schönsee at the Frau's prosperous farm.

References? Her laughter rang out, scattering the birds

on the fence. Yes. Olga had references from Frau Reinhardt Krause herself. Everyone knew about Dr. Krause, head of the German Christians. "One People, One Reich, One Faith," cried Olga, her words carrying in the wind.

The Nazi songs she sang as she rode fortified her spirit. Why need she be afraid of an old Mennonite woman? Olga was prepared for her interview. Where did these strange people hail from anyway? She'd read that though they were of Dutch extraction, they long ago adopted German ways and called themselves good Germans.

Gerhard put down his newspaper, the *Völkischer Beobachter* (national observer), which kept him abreast of the Reich plans for finding lands for its German citizens and guaranteeing their care under the love of Führer Hitler. Automatically he rubbed his thumb against his forefinger. Then he caught himself. *Esther always teases me*, he thought, *about my thumb and forefinger*. "Ought to have been a watch repairman," she'd say, chidingly.

Seeing Olga's buggy rolling up the lane, Gerhard strode out on the porch to take charge of the horse while Olga and Esther had their interview.

"Heil Hitler!" Olga's raspy voice rose in a shout. Her fat hand extended in a salute. "I presume you're Herr Claassen?"

Herr Gerhard Claassen gave a halfhearted salute to the heavyset girl who had greeted him. "Heil Hitler," he said. Maybe he should have responded with the same force as her salute. But Gerhard was more interested in reading and reflecting. "Should never have been a farmer," Esther told him.

Olga tossed him the reins as she leapt heavily from the tilting buggy.

Esther brushed her auburn hair with her fine-boned hand. Her lean tallness gave her dignity. The tailored blue dress with long sleeves added an elegance for a farmer's wife. It was easy to see prosperity here—in their clothing, in the imposing two-story white house.

"Oh, I wish Violet could have stayed," Esther said to Gerhard, not knowing he was already outside.

Nevertheless, this woman stepping up on the porch said she had references. On the phone her voice had resounded with strength. Esther remembered Olga even laughed heartily when asked if she got along well with boys. Esther wanted Chris, especially, to like whomever she hired. Hermann was past that age now, on his way to enter the Führer's service.

"Frau Claassen?" Olga didn't wait for Esther's hand. "Heil Hitler!" Again she issued her formal, brisk salute. Olga stared at the tall, attractive woman with the glowing hair done in a French roll. *A woman of substance*, she thought to herself.

"Fräulein Fritzenheimer? I'm so glad to meet you." Esther omitted the "Heil Hitler." It seemed such a bother, especially way out here in the country while interviewing a new domestic worker.

Esther smiled, looking straight into the light blue eyes of the woman staring at her. She greeted Olga with a friendly handclasp.

The smile disappeared from Olga's face. She clicked her heels. Her fat thighs slid together. Her arm flashed in Esther's face. "Heil Hitler, Frau Claassen!"

So this was the way it was. A dedicated one. If Hermann were here, he would appreciate this, Esther thought. She gave a half-salute, "Heil Hitler." Esther's innards tightened. She felt a chill at her neck. Olga had been the only applicant she could find. Everyone was in service to the Fatherland in one way or another. Freedom to change jobs was restricted by the Führer.

Olga sank heavily onto the horsehair couch. "Let me

bring in some tea before we discuss the position," said Esther, excusing herself and striding into the kitchen. She didn't say it, but a part of Esther knew it would have been a good time to roll out some dough with her heaviest rolling pin.

The freshly baked snickerdoodle cookie melted in Olga's mouth as she swished it down with the fragrant mint tea. "Four in your household, Frau Claassen? No problem at all. In my previous position, Herr Doctor and Frau Krause had seven children. They soon were marching with bright smiles under my guidance. No problems at all, Frau Claassen, no problems at all. In fact," Olga reached for another cookie, "Frau Krause wrote in my papers that I was best with boys." She handed Esther the envelope with her reference letter.

"Thank you." Esther took a moment to unfold the heavy sheet of paper. Frau Krause had written, "Olga Fritzenheimer embodies the best of the modern German young woman. Her many skills enable her to keep a home spotlessly clean. My daughters learned to make their beds and no longer neglected their studies under her watchful eye. My sons practically marched in perfection under her command. Olga Fritzenheimer is a dedicated daughter of our beloved Führer. Her recommendation from me is the highest."

Esther swallowed, placing the letter back in the envelope. Strong. Forceful. For a moment she studied the heavy girl whose arm was stretched over the back of her couch. *She certainly makes herself at home,* she thought.

They toured the spacious house together. Entering Christian's room, Olga's face spread in a happy smile. "What a faithful son your boy must be." Her quick eye surveyed the open notebook on his desk, where he made his daily Hitler Youth activity entries.

"A bookcase. When I have my work done, Frau Claassen, Christian and I can read together." She strained to catch the titles of the books on the shelf. The only one she could read was by someone named London.

"I see your sons revere our beloved Führer," Olga smiled widely as she spied the framed print of Hitler on the wall above the bed.

Esther explained the weekly routines—washing on Monday, ironing on Tuesday, gardening with Esther on Wednesday, baking on Thursday, housecleaning on Friday, marketing on Saturday.

"My day off, Frau Claassen . . . since I'm Lutheran, I prefer the Sabbath as my day off. I would be among my people and attend the services in the village." Olga dipped her heavy head as if she were nodding piously at the closing of the prayer book reading.

Reasonable. If Esther didn't give her Sunday off, she'd have to take another day.

Esther was glad, after the house tour, that Gerhard entered the kitchen. They sat at the wide ash table, looking out the window over the garden.

"Gerhardt, Fräulein Olga brought excellent recommendations from Frau and Herr Doctor Krause. I've told her of the duties here. I've shown her the maid's room. Perhaps you have something to say?"

"If you are pleased with the Fräulein's recommendations, and"—his brown eyes held Olga's for a moment—"if you, Fräulein Olga, understand Frau Claassen's expectations and find the duties compatible, the two of you agree as you like." He reached into his pocket for his penknife, rubbing it with his long fingers.

So like Gerhard, thought Esther. She would have appreciated a moment alone with him. If she allowed the girl to go back to Tiegenhof without a contract, she might take a job somewhere else.

Just then Olga announced, "Frau and Herr Claassen, I

failed to inform you that Frau Goossen and Frau Bartel in the village of Schönsee expect me this afternoon if I do not contract with you."

That clinched it. Esther's serious face focused momentarily on her husband. Their eyes met. Where could she turn for another applicant? Gerhard didn't nod, but his friendly eyes seemed to say, "Do what you think is best; I have no objections." He removed the amber-colored knife from his pocket.

Receiving the nod and handshake from Frau Claassen, Olga lurched to her feet, heavy breasts swinging beneath her salute. Her hearty "Heil Hitler" announced her agreement to the Claassens' terms.

3

Wednesday, two weeks later, the three of them bent over their hoes in the garden. Chris, who was helping his mother and Olga in the garden, looked forward eagerly to his march in the afternoon with the Hitler Youth. He made certain that he carefully weeded three rows to his mother's and Olga's two. His sharp hoe raked through the flat-headed cabbages as the sweat dripped from his upper lip.

"I like her," he told his mother, a few days after Olga Fritzenheimer settled in. "She plans to go through my books with me. She promised to help me with the history of the Aryan race and our noble Fatherland."

So far Esther couldn't complain. Never had her copper pots shone so brightly from the hooks above the black stove. Olga's heaviness didn't slow her down. Esther had worried about that. But Esther herself couldn't scour the soap ring from the bathtub as briskly as Olga did.

Esther did think it strange that, with money being tight in the Fatherland, Olga splurged on the taxis that brought her and her many bags out to the farm. Olga had taken the horse and buggy before. *Maybe she is celebrating her achievement*, thought Esther.

23

Esther appreciated the way Olga slid that new electric iron across Christian's uniform, ironing his Hitler Youth shirt and pants to perfection. The uniform hung on his closet door, the swastika band carefully mounted on the sleeve. She wished, though, that Christian wasn't so emotional about that swastika emblem.

Olga's broad back was bent and her wide posterior turned up like a peasant woman in a Van Gogh charcoal, but her iron-solid body didn't shake with the vigorous scrapings of her hoe in the potatoes. "You'll be leaving for your doctor's appointment in Danzig tomorrow, Frau Claassen?"

"Yes, Olga. My yearly appointment with Doctor Rosenbaum. We take the train from Tiegenhof to Danzig, make a full day and as much of a holiday as we can. Chris likes the train ride. His father may take him to a moving picture in a theater there." She straightened, leaning on her hoe.

Olga finished her potato row and wiped sweat from her red cheek with the back of her arm. "The boy should be able to see one of the new German movies, approved by Herr Goebbel's Reich Chamber of Culture. None of those rotten American movies or the worthless French ones for the boy."

Olga stopped hoeing for a moment. She smiled over at Christian, who had finished the last of the cabbages. "I'll bake your usual four loaves of *Brot* (bread) and the pies you decide on, maybe some of those cookies Chris likes so well, Frau Claassen. When I finish that, if time permits, I'll start cleaning the two boys' rooms upstairs."

Glancing at Esther, Olga caught an approving nod. Surely it wouldn't take the whole day to do the baking, unless Frau Claassen wanted her to bake one of those difficult Dutch recipes she talked about.

"Good health to you, Frau Claassen, from the doctor. What did you say his name was? Rosenbaum?"

Esther leaned on her hoe handle for a moment, glad for the fresh breeze cooling her brow. "Rosenbaum, Doctor Isaac Rosenbaum. A specialist. Ever since Christian was born, Gerhard has insisted I stay with the doctor for my yearly checkup, He insists doctors in our small towns around here can't match Dr. Rosenbaum's skill."

Esther didn't think about it at first—Olga's silence as she bent, returning to her weeding.

But after a few more scrapes with the hoe, Esther heard Olga mutter, "Rosenbaum? Rosenbaum? Certainly isn't German, is it, Frau Claassen? And according to our Führer, all Jewish males must give their middle name as *Israel.* You mean you're going to Danzig to see Doctor Isaac *Israel* Rosenbaum, don't you Frau Claassen?"

Again Esther leaned on her hoe. She stared with blue-green eyes at the woman who, no doubt about it, was carrying out her duties with diligence. Why did she feel Olga was correcting her?

Then too there had been their discussion after Olga arrived late Sunday night from her day with the Lutherans in the village.

"A traitor in the church. Martin Niemöller is a guiding spirit of the Lutheran church. You have his book, *From U-Boat to Pulpit,* don't you, Frau Claassen? A best seller, singled out for special praise in the Nazi press. I can even quote from Pastor Niemöller: 'The Nazi revolution has finally triumphed and brought about the national revival for which I longed.' But yesterday Pastor Niemöller was denounced as an enemy of the Reich Bishop of the German Christians."

Gerhardt cleared his throat, getting ready to slip in a few words, but Olga's piercing voice continued. "You know, Herr Claassen, that Martin Luther had it right long ago: 'Rid the Jews of cash and jewelry, set their synagogues and schools on fire, put the complaining people in confinement in sheds and barns. Why should we listen to them howl?' "

Both Gerhard and Esther stood in the middle of the living room, frozen to the floor. They had no idea how to respond to the new maid with the swinging hand.

Trying to ease the situation and calm Olga, Esther opened her mouth. Now, afterward, she wondered whether she had spoken wisely.

"Well, Olga, our own denomination, the West Prussian Mennonites, honored the Führer. Our own paper, *The Mennonitische Blätter* (Mennonite newspaper), carried the story of our conference at Tiegenhagen, how in honor of the Führer's rise to the throne they sent their support and greetings."

Olga dropped her arm. Her eyes were intoxicated with ferver.

"I remember the Bible verse they sent the Führer, a favorite of one of our former leaders, Menno Simons: *For other foundation can no man lay than that is laid, which is Jesus Christ.* Our conference vowed cheerful cooperation for the rebuilding of the Fatherland. The Führer himself returned the greeting, thanking them for their spirit of cooperation." Esther wondered if she should have shared all of that. Her fingers toyed with her dress collar.

Olga cried triumphantly, "Then we're comrades together, all of us. *One People, One Reich, One Faith.*"

4

Chris leaned forward in his seat as the train rolled across the flat lands of the Werder, fertile farmlands reclaimed from marsh by his forefathers decades before. "Father, look at all the windmills. Oh, the seagulls!"

A smile touched Esther's lips at seeing the boy so pleased at this excursion. Combining a medical appointment in Danzig with a holiday always proved rewarding for them all.

"I would like to drive over to Elbing to see Aunt Christina sometime," commented Esther, reaching for Gerhard's warm hand. She glanced northward toward the city as the spire of St. Martin Church rose above the flat land.

Actually their own farm was on the Werder, an island between the Vistula on the west, the Nogat on the south, north and east, and the Gulf of Danzig to the north.

Dikes and drainage ditches crisscrossed the land. Here and there glimpses of villages in the lowlands of the Vistula-Nogat Delta flashed before them. Green, green all around beneath the blue of the sky. Trees planted decades before rose along the dikes. Reeds and bushes swayed in the wind at the edges of the wide, fertile fields.

Not all their people had stayed on the swampy farms. The cities of Danzig, Elbing, Graudenz, and Marienburg, with its famous castle now taken over by the Führer as an elite school for Advanced Hitler Youth—anchored the fertile delta lands to the earth.

"Our people are in all the cities," Gerhard commented. "Many of them in Danzig were merchants, traders, shippers, establishing themselves more than a hundred years ago."

"I remember Uncle Oscar," Chris said, turning to his father. "When I had my eighth birthday, he gave me a watch chain and told me I should wear it the day I got married."

They all laughed. But it was an expensive gold chain Oscar Penner had given him, and it was secure in the bureau in Chris's bedroom.

"If time permits, after the movie and after your mother's appointment with Dr. Rosenbaum, we will pay Uncle Oscar a visit," said Gerhard. "But we can't miss our train back, have to watch our time."

That was the way with Gerhard, winsome and engaging with a smile on his face. Even though he was a successful manager of his farm who oversaw two hired men and provided for their families, he wondered how it would have been had he gone to one of these cities in his youth. Would he have been a university professor like Cousin Aaron? A merchant, perhaps? But there had been the Great War, and many young men's plans had crumbled.

Esther sometimes called Gerhard a freethinker, more inclined to his own ideas of right and wrong. She had noted long ago that Gerhard was not as religious as she. That didn't make him a man of no faith, though, she thought now as she held his hand. Gerhard took his place in their congregation, the Ladekopp Mennonite Church. Established in 1735, it was a branch of the Grosswerder congregation of the 1600s, which grew too large and branched out into four congregations.

Gerhard liked to claim that there really was no reason for their being distinct as a separate church. "Our beliefs are not at all contrary to other Protestants around us, and we have a lot in common with the Catholics."

However, lately, with the establishment of the Reich Bishop, Esther had noticed Gerhard drawing back. She could tell he was not comfortable with the leanings of the churches and did not understand where Herr Hitler was leading.

Nevertheless, she'd always said, "Being German is important to Gerhard."

Esther tightened her fingers over his warm hand. His masculinity was heightened as he leaned forward in his spotless serge suit and blue tie. His brown moustache spread across his lip, not bunched and cropped like the Führer's. Many men were copying the Führer's moustache these days.

Gerhard withdrew his hand. He didn't want to mention it to Esther and the boy, but he had read in the evening paper that here, in August of 1939, German troops in spanking new uniforms were headed eastward from Berlin in moving vans, grocery trucks, and other vehicles.

But he knew it was no secret. The Führer was outraged that the Versailles Treaty made Danzig a "Free City." "Let it be returned to the Fatherland!" shrieked Herr Hitler. Everyone knew where the Führer stood on that issue. Few Germans disagreed with him. Gerhard hadn't liked Hitler's annexation of Austria to Germany two years ago but he no longer talked about it. "It's not the land, we need the land. It's the way it was done and the treatment of the people, especially Jewish people," he had said.

Anyway, Germany and Russia had signed a non-aggression pact. Peace. No more Great Wars. But why did

England and France so obstinately argue with the Führer's government? Time would tell. Peace would prevail. The Führer and his Reichstag (parliament) promised.

The train snaked into the outskirts of Danzig, once proud and Polish, now largely a German city though actually a "Free City."

"But wouldn't it be better if Danzig and its surrounding lands were brought back into the fold of the Fatherland?" asked many German people.

"Father, the spire—no, two of them." said Chris as he pointed.

"That one on the left is the spire of the St. Mary Church, one of the largest in the world. We'll be passing right by it on our way to Dr. Rosenbaum's office." Gerhard too leaned forward.

"The other one farther to the left is the spire of the town hall. Can you see the statue of Sigismund II on the top? He was king of Poland years ago. That spire rises up 269 feet."

They always felt safe coming to Danzig, with its Mennonite, Catholic, Lutheran, and other Protestant congregations. However, the Volkstag (Danzig legislative assembly) of the German government outlawed the Catholic Party and the Communist Party in Danzig. It was no secret to Gerhard that the Nazis were in power in the city, holding at least thirty-eight seats in the legislature.

The rush of the city engulfed them as they disembarked in the grand station. Neon lights flashed from marquees of theaters constructed after the Great War, when most of the city had been demolished.

"Time for our movie, Father? I can hardly wait."

"Yes, Christian, you and your father go on to the movie, and I hope it is a good one. I'm going to do some shopping. We don't have stores like these back in the country. Shall we meet at The Mariner for a seafood lunch?"

Gerhard and Chris agreed. "Now which movie shall we see?" Both man and boy gazed up and down the streets at the marquees. *Ein Tag mit den kleinen Mädchen* (A day with the little maidens) read one in dazzling blue. *Hans und das Bund Deutscher Mädel* (Hans and the league of German maidens), flashed another.

"Let's see that one," cried Chris, pointing to the heavy marquee which read *Jungvolk und das Land des Führer* (Youth guard and the country of the leader [Hitler]).

Limited by choices and by time, Gerhard paid the modest fee. They settled into the darkened theater. The crowd was sparse. "Oh, I hope it's good." Chris, like all boys his age, could scarcely wait until the film began.

The theater darkened. First there was the newsreel. And what news! The immoral French in their decaying society were worried about their line of defense against the Fatherland should there be a war. The fascist Communists plundered the cities of western Russia, persecuting the beloved German people there. The folly of what was called the British Army flashed before them—the pale, sickly faces of British soldiers trying to stand straight with their caved-in chests, rotting teeth showing through their smiles.

Then the feature. But it was dull. Chris twisted in his seat and Gerhard went to sleep. The movie droned on with no plot at all. Chris heard the same themes daily at his school and at his Hitler Youth meetings.

"This doesn't make me feel like I'm in a big city at all," he whispered to his nodding father. Soon there were other noises above his whispering, sounds of hissing and booing as the tired and bored audience began openly to make fun of the Nazi movie. A tall, sour-looking manager slipped to the edge of the stage, signaling for quiet, pointing to the large swastika-bedecked flag in the corner.

They were relieved to be on the street again in the

brisk sea air of the city. The intoxication of the change from farm to city engulfed them. Extravagant merchandise, opulently displayed in shop windows, tempted them. Long-legged *Fräulein* (young ladies) in expensive dresses and silk hose swung confidently by, cigarettes in their red-nailed fingers.

Here and there an immaculately groomed German officer or soldier smiled or saluted a "Heil Hitler" to comrades as they slid through the door of a cabaret. Mellow music and laughter floated out, along with the sultry voice of Marlina Dietrich on a recording.

They had to hurry with the bountiful seafood lunch, served graciously and in style. Esther's appointment at two o'clock nudged them on.

Old women in dark uniforms swept and polished the cobblestone as they entered the doorway and took the long flight of steps. Esther's face tightened. Everywhere in the area signs were posted in windows: *Juden unerwünscht* (Jews not welcome).

Such views regarding Jews weren't new. But had it come to this? In the window below Dr. Rosenbaum's office?

Relieved that the doctor's office door opened, Esther took a seat on an upholstered chair across from the polished door. Chris and Gerhard seated themselves on the horsehair couch.

What was wrong? At previous appointments, Esther had never been the only patient. Her eyes focused on Gerhardt, reflecting consternation. Silence engulfed them. Suddenly there was a footstep, then the mahogany door slowly opened.

"Frau Claassen, I'm glad to see you. You're looking well. And Herr Gerhard. And my, oh, my, is this Christian?"

His soft hand, the hand of a skilled physician, greeted

them all. "I'm going to put you in this other small waiting room with some books and magazines, Chris, while I examine your mother. My, how you've grown." The thin doctor lightly stroked the boy's blond hair.

Gerhard sat with Esther in the examining room. Such silence. Why did the doctor look so tired and thin?

With skilled eye and hand, he began his examination of Esther. "Frau Claassen, you have managed to keep well," he said, lowering his stethoscope. "Blood pressure normal. No signs of the complications you had after Christian was born." He inquired about her energy level or any unusual tiredness.

"No time for a blood test today, Frau Claassen. However, based on how you are doing and your appearance today, I'm going to send you home only with these iron supplement tablets. Congratulations, Herr Gerhard, for taking such good care of her." He smiled, easing himself into his chair.

"Herr Doctor, are *you* well?" Esther couldn't help but ask.

"Oh, Frau and Herr Gerhard, so much, so very, very much. . . . I cannot tell you all now, someday, someday—" his voice faded. His face had the look of old Abraham struggling up Mount Moriah to sacrifice Isaac.

5

"**H**err and Frau, Claassen, there's something I'm going to ask you to do. It is not by accident that you are the only patient here and the last one of the day, Frau Claassen."

The doctor's thin hand trembled as he held it before them.

"My wife, Rachael, and I made the decision after a lot of thought that this is what we must do. That was before the Gestapo (secret police) came for Rachael and Aaron, my son, last week before I arrived home from the hospital. Only God knows. They may be on a train for Auschwitz, they may be in prison here. They simply disappeared. My daughter, Ruth, hid herself in the attic. Merciful God."

Esther's eyes opened in shock as the horror of the doctor's words settled on her. She tried to speak but could not make a sound.

"Herr and Frau, I have known you people for many years. You are good people. I know of your faith, and I feel you are people of my own heart." He rose, his body at least forty pounds lighter than when they had seen him last. Opening an inner door, he said in a soft voice, "Ruth, my daughter, come here."

Taking her slender hand, he led the fourteen-year-old Jewish girl into the room. "This is our beloved Ruth, named after Ruth in the Bible who said, 'Your people shall be my people.' You must take Ruth with you back to your farm near Tiegenhof. I pray she will be safe with you, Frau Claassen. Otherwise, she will perish."

It was as if the last wind of all time had ceased at a long forgotten coast and the sea settled in perpetual stillness.

Esther and Gerhard rose, tears in their eyes. "Oh, my child, my child." Esther reached out with her sun-tanned hands, clasping the hand of the girl whose eyes were like liquid pools.

"Oh, Doctor Rosenbaum, Doctor Rosenbaum! What can we say," Gerhard gasped before a sob choked him. Tears streamed down his face. An almost unbearable grief hung in the air.

"How lovely she is, how beautiful." Esther's mother eyes surveyed the girl standing before her, her long hair parted on the side, swept back. The street dress she wore was smart and new with white trimming. Her expensive shoes gleamed on her small feet.

"Your packages, my daughter," said Dr. Rosenbaum, reaching in a closet and setting them out on a chair. "I've wrapped your clothes in packages as if you'd just been shopping. This one is your violin. No one will think it is luggage. You must go with the Claassens to their farm, to their community, my daughter."

Dr. Rosenbaum knew that it was God above who gave him the strength to do what he was now doing. He had prayed before that his body and soul might stay together until this hour passed. God now honored his prayer.

"*Shema*, Israel," prayed Dr. Rosenbaum. "Hear, O Israel, the Lord is One." His eyes were closed and his lifted hand, held by unseen angels, blessed his daughter, blessed God, and blessed Gerhard and Esther.

"Oh, Father, my father!" sobbed the slender daughter. "Must I leave you, is there no other way? When will we see Mother and Aaron?"

"Hush, my child. God decrees it. Part with my blessing and the blessing of Israel. Oh my beloved daughter! Remember the God of these people is our God and that Jesus himself was a Jew. You will be safe in their home. God will watch over all our family. My prayers will—" Then Dr. Rosenbaum sobbed, bent over, crying, "Oh, my God, my God!"

Then, controlling himself he directed, "Bring in your son Christian. My boy, come in. Now go, all of you. Who knows who is listening or when the Gestapo will knock down this door? Go, go, oh, blessed people."

"But you, you, Doctor Rosenbaum, what about—"

He cut her off, his hands on their backs, "Go. Go at once. I must tell no one about myself, no one. Shalom."

The door closed behind the four heartbroken ones as he slumped to the floor, weeping.

6

The old hired man, Otto Slavanski, never understood how he confused folks when he'd say, "I'm half Gypsy, half Polish, and half Jewish."

"Otto, you're a man-and-a-half!" folks called back to him, humoring him. His wife, Beulah, bumbling along in her work brogues and heavy stockings, tried to explain it to him, but his simple mind was unable to grasp it.

When the closed van roared down the road from Schönsee to the farm, he felt honored to see the six Brownshirts with nightsticks in their hands and faces set in grim lines. *Important military folks coming to have business with Herr Claassen,* he thought to himself.

It was only eight o'clock in the morning. The Brownshirts were so late because they had been busy since midnight dragging from their beds the pitiful folks of the hinterlands who did not meet the qualifications to live in the Führer's purified land. It was always better to jerk them from their beds at night. They resisted less when their minds were befogged and confused. Then, too, the Brownshirts could laugh and hoot as the beggarly criminals who refused to honor the Führer pleaded not to have· their throats cut and groveled at the Brownshirts' feet.

They had been so successful this night that they had extended their hours to come out to this farm.

Since 1935 they had been outlawed—Jews, Gypsies, pacifists, the unfortunate ones with below-average mental capacities, the insane in the institutions, or any who spoke against the Führer's noble objectives and brilliant strategies for bringing in a new world order under the leadership of the German people.

Old Otto bent over the hog trough, enjoying the grunts and smackings of the pigs as they ate their grain and swilled the slops. He lifted his head to watch the six smart Brownshirts hurry up the lane.

Only thing, instead of heading to the house for a visit with Herr Claassen, they marched vigorously toward the pigpen.

Fear seized Otto. His face showed his terror and he trembled in a feeble attempt to smile at the powerful men tromping toward him. But before he could get out so much as a grunt, whack! A blow of a nightstick descended on his head, knocking his Polish cap into the mire.

Another callous, brutal Brownshirt eagerly joined the fray. Raucous laughter ascended. "Look at the old Polish Jew-Gypsy dance!" cried the tallest one with the long jaw and cold, gray eyes. "Protective custody for the feeble-minded," hollered the heavyset one, delivering more blows.

Otto, face now buried in the manure and muck, was nearly unconscious. He scarcely felt his body slam against the steel floor of the closed van. He could not see the terror-filled face of Beulah, who had dropped the bowl of turnips she had just pulled from her garden.

"My God! My God, where're they taking Otto?" She screamed, stumbling over her turnips as she ran to the big house. Maybe Olga could help. "Oh, God above, have mercy," she cried with uplifted arms.

But when she pounded on the kitchen door, Olga took her time, as she was busy mixing the bread dough, getting an early start on Frau Claassen's rolls and loaves. When she finally wiped her hands and strode to the door, a frown creased her forehead. "Beulah Slavanski, you don't have to knock the house down. Such a fracas! What are you blubbering about?"

She opened the screen a crack. After all, there was not time, with all her duties, Frau Claassen gone this day to Danzig and all, to pass the time of day with a dirty peasant woman named *Slavanski*.

"Oh, Olga, Olga, they've taken Otto." The woman shook and sobbed, wiping her tears with a hand dirtied by the soil and turnips. "Help me, Olga! Where have they taken him, what am I to do?" Her pitiful plea came from the bottom of her soul.

Olga stared at the woman twisting on her ankles, weeping and wringing her hands. Better not let her in the house, have trouble getting her out; besides, Olga didn't want her tracking up the kitchen floor.

"It will come out all right, you'll see. You'll see. They are only doing it for the Fatherland and for the Führer. I know you don't understand now, Beulah." How she hated saying that name. She despised it about as much as the name Slavanski.

"It's only for his protection—protective custody, they call it. Not for you to understand. Go back and hoe your turnips. It will probably be over before sundown, and your hairy man will want to climb in bed with you come night. Go on back." Olga hooked the door and turned back to her dough.

That afternoon, toward sunset, the surrey rocked down the dirt road toward the farmstead.

What shall I tell the folks of the community? How shall I tell them? How shall we keep her? Must we keep her hidden? Oh, my God! The questions whirled through Esther's brain as they swayed in the surrey behind the plodding draft horse, Major.

Now pale, Ruth sank back, allowing her shoulder the comfort of Esther's warm side. In the front seat, Gerhard and Chris rode in silence. The moan of the wind through a hedge along the road accompanied the unspoken moan in their hearts.

"We must recognize what is," Gerhard whispered, slapping the reins over old Major's broad rump.

"Thank God, we have Olga to help us. Olga is so organized, she will guide us. These young Germans know more of what is happening in our land." Esther smiled through eyes still wet with tears for the sorrowing Ruth, her bundles beside her and at her feet.

"What is going to happen to Doctor Rosenbaum?" asked Chris, bewildered by the tragic turn of the day.

"Son, we must pray that God will take care of Doctor Rosenbaum and," he added, "give us help and guidance."

As the surrey rocked, Gerhard pondered what he had heard over the Reich broadcasting system. "The savior, Herr Hitler, stopped our national humiliation by ending the despised Weimar government."

The tough speeches of the Führer seemed to appeal to the good and decent in a person. *Don't they?* Gerhard continued to think.

But the new Law of Coordination, which dumped Chancellor Weimar's democratic government and shoved in the Führer government, was a problem. All civil servants, all judges, all teachers, even some clergy were replaced by those dedicated to the Führer.

But what happened to all those shoved aside to make room for the Nazis who took their places? Where were they now?

The names of those camps. What did they call them? Concentration camps? Such names—Dachau, Sachsenhausen, Ravensbrück, Buchenwald, Auschwitz, and, twenty miles from their farm, Stutthof. It was good to have factories like those where the criminals and betrayers of Germany could work and make a decent contribution to the Fatherland, wasn't it? Esther never wanted to talk about it. But now, Gerhard had to admit, he was as frightened as she. But then, *no one* talked about it.

Who was watching them, even now? Could the Gestapo be in Schönsee and in Tiegenhof? Was it really just another cross on a country's flag, or was it truly the poisonous spider?

"Gerhard, Chris," said Esther, leaning forward. "We must decide what we shall call her. Her name. Who shall we say Ruth is?"

Now that was a problem. Disastrous, wouldn't it be, to drag this young Jewish girl into Tiegenhof, or into their own church come Sunday, surrounded by their very own people, and say, "This is Doctor Rosenbaum's daughter, Ruth Rosenbaum."

"Let's call her Ruth, Cousin Ruth. . . ." Esther's mind searched. Then she remembered. "Ruth Schwartzentruber. Her name is Ruth Schwartzentruber. You know, Gerhard, those South German Amish Mennonites and the Swiss— many Schwartzentrubers. And did you ever see a single one who was not dark and black-haired?"

"Come to think of it," agreed Gerhard, "I believe you're right. Schwartzentruber men . . . all dark-complexioned and hairy."

Ruth rocked in the surrey, giving herself over to these people and to forces now beyond her control. She whispered her father's prayer: *"Shema,* Israel, the Lord thy God is one."

By the time the surrey pulled into the lane, a gray mist

had settled in from the sea. The trees leaned from the easterly wind as darkness settled. Esther pulled a shawl around her shoulders. But they all needed shawls, for the chilly wind blowing over the Werder lowlands was not to be compared to the icy cold now drifting over their spirits.

Heinrich Fitz, the second hired man in the cottage across from old Otto's, had already turned on the new electric lights in the barn. He coaxed old Molly and Wilhelmina into their stalls. He was scared, now that old Otto had been scooped up and trundled off.

And he grumbled at all the work left for him to do. "Always thought there was something fishy about that dirty Polish farmhand across the lane. Never did do more than pass the time of day with him," he mumbled. He himself was certain of his German roots, even if it did mean his job for the Führer was only as a hand on Herr Claassen's farm.

Now the Claassens and their guest had to leave the fragile protection of the surrey. They'd rocked together, thought together, had silence and prayer together. Strange how in only one day such change could come about. They had started out from the warm hearth of house and Fatherland, and returned at sunset to their own house, disembarking like refugees on a strange shore.

Esther led Ruth, who stood tall, clasping two of her bundles and allowing Chris to carry the others.

"This is our home, my dear child; you are welcome." The girl surveyed the large farmhouse and the glow of the lights from the windows. She must obey her father. *Your people shall be my people.* Ruth held back a sob. There were no more tears. Her slender foot touched the boards of the porch.

"Olga. We're home, Olga!"

7

Cousin Ruth *Schwartzentruber* from South Germany was a quick learner. In spite of Olga's direct and commanding way, Ruth was determined to carry her load. Besides her beloved violin, she had one other love—cooking. Before her Grandmother Elsa died, she had learned some of the old Yiddish recipes. Now, in the middle of situations so far beyond her control, she vowed to do her part.

Frau Esther had taken her aside in the upstairs bedroom and said, "It's best, dear Ruth, not even to mention the Yiddish recipes." It was heartbreaking and nearly impossible, trying to put a lid on your past. She prayed she wouldn't let something leak by being careless.

"Where do you keep the onions?" she asked, as she removed the boiled potatoes from the stove. In her attempt to learn from and to assist the busy Olga, she had volunteered to make the German potato salad.

"Onions are in the pantry. You must be careful and follow the recipe. Too much onion and the salad is spoiled," called Olga, who was shredding cabbage for the borscht. Olga didn't trust anyone in her kitchen who played the violin, anyway. Olga decided she'd need to review with Frau

Claassen her own precise duties and just when someone else was stepping over the line.

"My own mother made borscht too, Olga, but it was different. She used red beets and fresh cream. Before the meal, she served it chilled, with bright green herbs."

Ruth peeled back the outer layers on the golden onion. Better to work, to keep busy, otherwise she might fall into a bottomless pit of all the unknowns surrounding her.

Esther considered Ruth's willingness to help Olga in the kitchen a blessing. She wondered if it would be annoying for Olga, but Olga only tossed her bloody butcher knife on the cutting board and replied, "Long as I'm in charge. Long as I'm in charge."

Bringing in a bouquet from the asters she'd planted alongside the front veranda, Esther began arranging them in her cut-glass vase. They planned a candlelight dinner tonight, using the best china and her grandmother's silver. In a couple of hours, Hermann would be stepping in here all bright-eyed in his new uniform, back from Nuremberg.

She thought of her broad-shouldered son, his strong jaw so clean-shaven. Dark-skinned too, like Ruth. It ran on Gerhard's side. One of his grandparents, which one she had forgotten, was South German, from the old Swiss lineage. Dark-skinned like those Schwartzentrubers they'd discussed that terrible day in the surrey.

Esther rose early to have time to read from the Psalms and to bow her head and pray in the early morning light. "He that keepeth Israel shall neither slumber nor sleep." The words brushed her heart and gave her comfort. How could anyone live through days like these without faith or prayer?

Last week she'd held poor old Beulah Slavanski, who was terrified and grief-stricken. "Oh Frau Esther, my Otto. My loving, kind Otto. Where is he? They've killed him, they've killed him."

Looking over the woman's graying head, Esther tried to comfort her. "My poor Beulah. We must hope and pray. I don't know the answers, Beulah, but I'll pray for Otto's return, and I'll care for you while we wait. Hush now, Beulah."

Then she had led Beulah through the herb and flower garden. They sat on the little stone bench, remembering other days, other hours when the earth was not breaking open so drastically beneath them.

So far they'd heard nothing from Otto, even though the very next day Gerhard had gone into the village to inquire of the mayor. All mayors of all villages, towns, and cities were loyal Nazis, carrying out the Führer's commands. The mayor would know.

"You'll have to go on to Tiegenhof, Herr Claassen," said Mayor Braun coldly. "Our court and jury offices are too small here. We do not handle cases of traitors and concerns of Jews and non-Germans."

So Gerhard parked Major and the buggy at the livery and boarded the train for Tiegenhof. Stepping down with the other travelers, he raced over to the Magistrate Court on Wilhelmsstrasse. But it was now called the *Volksgerichtshof* (people's court), the court commanded by the black-shirted *Schutzstaffel* (SS, protective squad).

After Gerhard had waited until three o'clock in the afternoon, a smirking Blackshirt clicked his boots and asked, "Herr Claassen, you are of the Mennonites, aren't you? Your hired man, Otto Slavanski? Only record here states that he is among those who are either insane or feebleminded. He has been given the proper treatment for such under the Führer's leadership and wisdom."

That was all. Gerhard was dismissed. The icy blast of the reception at the court chilled his bones. The first question, "You are of the Mennonites, aren't you?" shook him to his toes.

When he arrived back at the farm, Esther escorted him upstairs, bringing him a cup of hot brandy and coffee. They sat in their closed room, bewildered, comforting each other.

They tried to shove aside the fear and pain. After all, this should be a joyous day. Maybe the last of the days when Hermann could come and go, now that he was in Herr Hitler's *Reichswehr* (defense force).

Esther placed the asters in the center of the table and glanced past the veranda. "He's coming up the lane! Hermann's returned from Nuremberg."

But her heart ached as her gallant son stepped high in shiny boots and handsome uniform of the Führer's army. She brushed a wisp of hair and ran to the front door to greet him.

After scrubbing the bloody cutting board and knife, Olga had shoved them aside. Striding in to check the tablecloth on the long table, she saw Frau Claassen down the lane with her new soldier boy, Hermann. Olga studied them. It was clear that Frau Esther was detaining him. Why did he look so bewildered? What was so important that Frau Esther needed to gallop down the lane and halt her boy in his tracks to explain?

8

Hermann, back straight, hair parted on the side, sat proudly in his army uniform at the table loaded with his favorite foods. The warmth of his father to the right and of his beloved mother at the opposite end pleased him. Admiration beamed from brother Chris, sitting beside him.

And the new *cousin*? Ruth sat in modest silence opposite Chris, with her back to the windows which framed the sunset. From time to time, her magical fingers brushed a wisp of that dark hair from her forehead.

"For this bountiful supply, for your watchful care over us, and for the love around our table, we give you thanks," Gerhard prayed.

Esther started the fresh baked rolls, followed by the butter churned by Ruth. Olga, ruddy face poised, handed the heavy platter to Gerhard. "Beef with sour gravy, Herr Claassen, made by the old recipe."

Olga took pride in her accomplishment. So far Frau Esther had only praised her. Heavy work load here. Added to the tasks now was that new girl, Ruth. Funny thing, when she asked Frau Esther about the length of the visit, why had she hedged like that?

At the end of the table Esther smiled, her warm eyes catching those of her sons, now one, now another. She would not let the pain at the edge of her heart spoil the dinner. Who knew? This might be the last time they could gather like this. And Ruth? Each time she looked at the lovely maiden from Danzig, she choked back a sob. "God give me strength to walk by faith," she prayed.

Christian leaned toward his brother, a morsel of beef on his fork, ready to speak. But Gerhard said, "Tell us about Nürnberg (Nuremberg), Hermann."

Olga leaned in the dining room doorway, noting the glow on the young man's face.

"Oh, Father, how can I describe it? Chris, I wish you could have been with me, but then, you shall have your day. We marched by the thousands into Zeppelin Field beneath hundred-foot eagles. How can I describe it?"

The Jewish girl opposite him lifted her head, her silky hair swept behind a shoulder. "I was at the art gallery in Nürnberg, once when—" Her voice faded.

"It is an old city, Cousin Ruth."

Esther looked from Hermann to Ruth. They'd gotten off to a good start. "Olga, the green beans, please."

Olga strode to the kitchen, "Yes, Frau Claassen. Indeed, time for the vegetables."

"Father, the new order of Germany is glorious. I'm so thankful I can be part of such an unsurpassed movement so for our Fatherland. And to hear the Führer, Father, to hear his voice. No wonder the clergy say that much of his thought and program are the same as that of the church. But you know more about that than I." Hermann turned to pass the bread plate, chanting,

Who reluctantly swims against the stream
Will become a partial man;
Who never meets the opposition
Will always stay in the dark band;
Therefore, push ahead; we are young contenders.

"My thoughts exactly. My thoughts exactly. We will honor the young man in the Reichswehr uniform," said Olga, handing him the Delft blue dish with the bacon and green beans. "Handsome soldier indeed in your family, Frau Claassen."

Their voices mingled above the clank of forks and knives against plates and dishes and the sipping of the wine from Grandmother Froese's crystal glasses.

"Mother, you would have gloried in the pageantry, the banners, the standards. Some said it was like the most splendid of the Catholic churches and the greatest mass."

Esther, laying down her fork, held her glass. Suddenly her appetite vanished. Nevertheless, she smiled through the mist of love for her son in her eyes.

"Father, you like marching music. You used to play the trumpet in the Schönsee band. The Führer's Reichswehr Band played the Badenweiler March as he entered with his noble assistants Herr Goering, Herr Hess, Herr Goebbels, and Herr Himmler. Oh, Chris, Cousin Ruth, could you only have been there to see them all in their glory!"

Christian leaned in so that his shoulder touched his fine-suited brother. Oh, to be like him!

Hermann's deep voice vibrated as he continued, holding them in rapt attention. "For four years, Herr Hitler explained, he has been preaching only peace, only peace. Oh, Mother, you sometimes play it on our piano, the Egmont Overture. When the orchestra began that, five thousand standards bearing the swastika rose into the light."

Hermann's eyes gleamed like the crystal wine decanter.

"I thought it was at night, that rally," said Chris.

"Oh, Christian, it was at night. A hundred and fifty searchlights, every forty feet, beaming into the air. When the light beams crossed in the sky at twenty-five thousand feet—oh, Mother, never have I been in such a cathedral of light." Hermann was overcome by the pageantry. Even now his spirit was enmeshed in the spiritual intoxication of that Nürnberg hour.

"Afterward we marched most of the night under fifteen thousand torchlights, beneath the swastikas and standards, singing the victorious Nazi anthems."

Olga, who had refilled the platter, leaned in. "More beef, Herr Hermann?" Her breast brushed his shoulder. She felt comradely warmth for him. She tightened her lips to keep from humming too loudly a hymn for the new German Faith Movement: "The time of the cross has gone now, the sunwheel shall arise. And so, with God, we shall be free at last, and give our people their honor back."

"I hope, my sons," Esther looked at one, then the other, "I hope you will not forget our simple ways, the ways of our forefathers who rescued this land from the sea—their songs, their ways."

Esther thought of the old confession of faith she had reread only yesterday, with its firm call to put away the sword. But now that had been explained in a new way. "Just-war theory," the clergy, including their own humble preachers at their meetinghouse, called it. Esther's slender hand, tanned from gardening, reached for her glass.

The dinner drew to a close. Gerhard knew of the intoxicating powers of uniforms, trumpets, flags, and banners. He himself had marched to the martial sounds of bands during the Great War. The shredded flesh and bloodied ground of the battlefield, however, sobered most soldiers. There were, though, those drunk from even the torn flesh and blood of battle. God help us.

"Mother, some music. Ruth, you play the violin. Come." Gerhard motioned with his large hand. "Let's sit in the parlor for some music. Come, Ruth." He stood, placing his fatherly hand on her shoulder.

"Let's help Olga clear the table. She must join us. Then we can have coffee and dessert," said Esther.

Esther sat at the old grand piano with spreading Queen Anne legs. Ruth, tossing her long hair, took her violin from its case and began to tune it to the key struck by Esther.

When the fine violin was in tune, the slender girl lifted it to her chin as Esther's fingers began an overture to the selection from *Midsummer Night's Dream*.

How regal, my wife, Gerhard thought to himself, studying Esther at the piano in the evening light. He loved her fragrant auburn hair, now braided and crowning her head. And Ruth, like a new daughter, so gifted too. The blessing of their music would heal the pain in their hearts.

Ordered by the Jewish girl's skilled fingers and bow, the violin began to weep into the twilight air, sobbing above the mellow harmony of the piano.

Olga, her squat body hunched at the edge of her chair, leaned in, face tightened in discernment. What was it? What sounds were those? Her cabbage head with its ungraceful hair cut tilted to one side.

Leaping from her chair, she waved her arm, "*Halten! Halten! Verboten! Verboten, verboten!*" (stop! forbidden!).

Lumbering to the piano, she jerked the sheet of music from in front of the shocked Esther and the terrified girl and ripped it to shreds.

"Verboten, verboten! You cannot play that Jewish man's music after this holy hour of honoring the Führer and your brave son of the Reichswehr. Mendelssohn, Mendelssohn, God in heaven," she clutched her fat head. "He's a vile Jew, an enemy of the Fatherland."

9

The air became more brittle in the Claassen household. Chris noticed the change most in his mother—that serious, pained look on her face. She seemed to rattle her pots and pans nervously. Was she really searching so much for the rolling pin? But then, it was hard to keep the secret about Ruth from Olga.

"Mother, do you have one of your headaches?" he inquired.

"No, no, son. Just thinking. So much to do. Such changes. When Ruth and I finish the embroidery on the pillowcases, why don't you and she take a walk out by the pond and read together under the willows."

Actually, she had changed the night Olga went on a rampage and tore up that sheet music. But it could be, too, that it was on account of Hermann, swept up in the Reichswehr and the radio news about how those decadent French were troubling the Führer. The Führer had to send in his troops to quell the vengeful Czechs and rescue the 3 million German people in that country.

Now there was talk of rescuing the German people in Poland for the Fatherland, saving them from the polluted Poles. Hitler felt sorrow for German people who had to live outside the bounds of the Fatherland.

Chris tried hard to sort it out from his book on *Rassenkunde* (racial science). Herr Bowman, his Hitler Youth instructor, lectured on it weekly. Is German blood really superior? If it were really proven, thought Chris, he'd go with it. He must support the truth of science. That was what was required of a good student—loyalty.

Ruth could quote both the Bible and Shakespeare, not to mention all those classical pieces she played on her violin. Then too, how could the Jews be so racially inferior if Ruth's father was an important Danzig doctor?

Yet it was the law to be in the Hitler Youth. And the "Heil Hitlers" they said with pride and vigor so many times daily demonstrated their commitment to Herr Hitler and the Fatherland.

He'd heard it himself on the radio: "I say your child belongs to me, to the Fatherland. You will pass on, but your child carries the pure blood of Germany. The Reich will give the youth to no one; they belong only to the Fatherland. We shall teach them, and Germany will reign for a thousand years."

The balmy south wind soothed them as they sat by the pond under the swaying willow wands. He didn't put it into thought or words, but a part of him recognized that the tension eased when he was outside in the sun and the wind or walking through the pasture.

Chris wanted to ask Ruth about being Jewish. But he guessed that it was forbidden, especially since many of the stores placed signs in their windows saying *Juden unerwünscht* (Jews not welcome).

"Do you really believe what you are reading in that book on racial science?" Ruth surprised him with the question.

"Why, why—" How could he answer? It was as if some organ he could not name twisted inside him. He brushed back his cowlick, his blue eyes focused on this Jewish girl who indeed was beautiful.

"Why, Ruth, I guess if it's printed in the books we study in our schools, it must be—" But his tongue seemed to hold itself, as if a hidden finger had touched it. A verse flashed into his mind, a verse his father read to them from the same Bible he heard read over the pulpit by Preacher Schroeder: "Wherein thou judgest another, thou condemnest thyself. . . . Glory, honor, and peace to every man that worketh good, to the Jew first, and also to the Gentile; for there is no respect of persons with God."

Chris was not fully conscious of his quick look back over his shoulder. Today was cleaning day; Olga was upstairs in the bedrooms.

"My mother doesn't believe the racial science books. Father doesn't say anything, but he reads those Bible verses. Then Preacher Schroeder preaches that we should obey the ones who govern over us because that is in keeping with the Bible."

Ruth reached for a tall stem of grass, gone to seed. She broke it, waving the spicy stem under her nose. "You don't really believe it, Chris. I can tell. You hesitate when you talk about it. Our people say you are the *goyim* (Gentiles), and are not in the will of God as we Jewish people. But," she added, "I don't believe it, that you are inferior to Jews. And I do believe that God loves Gentiles and Jews alike."

Ruth was old enough to realize that it would be disastrous if the discussion were overheard. Esther had cautioned her about Olga and how it was necessary to keep passing herself off as Cousin Ruth Schwartzentruber. Jews had had to flee and disguise themselves for hundreds of years. It was nothing new. Besides, she herself was good in drama.

Playing the role of a Mennonite girl from Switzerland wasn't hard at all—if she kept her wits about her. She'd do her best to win over Olga. But Christian? He was a lad of her own heart. Those Bible verses he quoted—well, maybe they could read from the Psalms together. Then too, she could review her Shakespeare, and they could read a play together—if they avoided *A Midsummer Night's Dream*.

It was painful for Chris, being twelve years old, sitting with this Jewish girl who was already fourteen. Only two years, but it might well have been a decade. She acted more like a grown woman than a girl. But look how she had suffered. That tragic day leaving her father's office. What ever happened to him? Should he bring it up? Could they talk about it? Chris felt a lump rising in his chest even thinking about it.

No. He'd better let Ruth bring it up if she wanted to talk about that day. He himself would surely mature all in one day if such disaster befell his family. It was hard enough seeing Hermann go off to the Reichswehr, even if Hermann was glad of it, rejoiced in it. The parting still pained. He knew his mother, especially, worried. Father had been in the Great War. He kept his feelings to himself.

Then too, Chris wanted to cry when he got back from Danzig that terrible day to find that the Brownshirts had loaded up old Otto. They had said that he was feeble-minded and that the Glorious New Order had no place for folks like him. It didn't seem right. He missed Otto.

A part of him wished the Führer would hurry and rescue the German people in Poland so it would all be over and they could live in peace in the new Fatherland.

"Christian! Ruth!" Esther's voice rang clear, carried by the summer wind. "Time for dinner." She meant lunch. All farm folks called the noon meal "dinner."

That afternoon Ruth and Esther started their embroidery project. Chris thought this was a good time to read that book he'd been saving all this time. Hermann had read it long ago and passed it on to him.

His bedroom was large, with wide southern windows letting in the breeze and warm sunlight. The chimney against the wall provided comforting heat on winter nights. A sadness swept over him. The room reminded him of Hermann and how they used to wrestle together on the rug and study the Hitler Jugend materials together.

Where was the book? He searched the top shelf where he had placed a few rocks, mementos of a wonderful day spent in the forest with the Hitler Youth (though he had returned with terrible blisters on his heels).

There were all his well-bound German Youth Studies books, his magazines, his Bible. Where was that Jack London book, *White Fang*? He'd started to read it last year and got sidetracked by all the record keeping, marching, and studies of school and Jugend.

Chris remembered the book. It was about a swashbuckling young man who sallied off to Alaska, to that godforsaken land. He couldn't remember just what for; he'd have to start over. It was also about a dog, the half-wild White Fang, who was caught between the world of Alaskan men and the snow and wild.

"Mother!" Chris called down the hall to the room where she and Ruth were working on the quilt. "Have you seen my book *White Fang*?

"No, son. I'm sure it's on your bookshelf. Look again. You know that boy takes after his father, impatient when it comes to finding his things."

Chris searched again, then hurried across the shiny oak floorboards to Hermann's room with the fabulous wallpaper. Surveying his bookcase, he was puzzled. "Where is it?"

"Mother, I can't find it."

Floorboards squeaked as heavy feet ascended the staircase. The bulky body of Olga with her unbecoming haircut stood before him, holding the book by the fascist Jack London of the United States. She held the book with two fingers, as if it were a poisonous toadstool.

"This what you're looking for? This?" She growled.

"A gift from Hermann? Poison!" Her pale eyes were filled with disdain. "I'm having a conference with Frau Esther and Herr Claassen just as soon as he returns from Tiegenhof. First a stranger in this house, settling in, increasing my workload, and no extra pay. Next scandalous music of a traitor Jew rising up before a noble young German soldier. Now a book." Her frown scalded Chris. "You are sneaking a book *verboten* in 1935 at the book-burning in Berlin."

She stuffed the evil volume beneath her apron, raised her head while turning her heavy body. "When I'm in Tiegenhof, I may have to have a meeting with a deputy from Herr Goebbels' office. We'll see, we'll see."

10

"We have to do something, Gerhard. Everything seems to be crumbling. Olga's threat against Chris yesterday over the book makes me too nervous."

Esther turned to Gerhard, who was sitting in the mauve upholstered chair in their bedroom by the double window.

"We all feel it, Esther." He slipped off his boots and began to unbutton his shirt. "Olga is heavy-handed for the Führer. Dedicated to the Fatherland. Yet look at the help she gives. No one can say she shirks her work."

"Yes. But having Ruth here without Olga knowing who she really is seems like a time bomb to me. It would be disastrous if Olga knew we were harboring a Jewish girl. Then too, we never know when Christian may let it slip."

Esther began to brush out her long auburn hair. She didn't put it into words, but they both knew the dilemma brought on by their consciences and what they really believed about Jewish people. Yet what they were doing was criminal. Himmler's army of Brownshirts, Blackshirts and the Gestapo (secret state police) roamed the land.

Yet wasn't it their beloved Germany that kept the murdering hordes of Russian Bolsheviks from taking over Europe? "Bolsheviks Make War on Our Beloved German People in the Ukraine," read the headlines. Pastor Schroeder heard through the grapevine that their own people were driven out into the frigid winds while their houses burned behind them in the Russian Ukraine.

Mennonite women stumbled in the dark, trying to find their children, while murderous thugs loaded up their husbands and hauled them off to dungeons and to mines in Siberia. To make matters worse, the Western powers sided with Russia. "Hitler is the evil," they said.

For several years now the Führer's Germany had sponsored resettling their own Mennonite groups from Russia to new lands in Paraguay. Even their own Herr Kliewer had traveled to Paraguay, that godforsaken land, to set up Hitler Youth Groups so the young people would not lose their identity. Those Russian Mennonites were of German blood, Germans saved from Stalin.

"Pastor Schroeder told Amos Goossen that the American Mennonites set up a refugee center in Berlin for these starving refugees fleeing Stalin," said Gerhard, slipping his blue pajama top over his broad chest.

"Gerhard, tomorrow I'm hitching Major to the spring wagon. I'll ride over to Pastor Schroeder's place." Elizabeth's hazel eyes fastened upon his weathered face. "I have to tell him about Ruth, who she really is. We cannot keep it from him. Let him decide about the rest of the folks in the church, whether they should know or not."

Gerhard reached out for Esther, and their hands clasped tightly.

Pastor Schroeder looked out of a window of his red-tiled house. "Why, here comes Esther Claassen up the walk. Myra, maybe you ought to make a pot of tea."

Pastor Schroeder seated Esther in the high-backed chair by his desk. He reached over to raise the green shade, letting in the morning light. My, Esther did look pained, he thought. But then, these days most folks in Germany appeared bewildered. News hadn't been exactly good—the aggressive Poles, the war-thirsty Russians, those immoral Western countries. Lowering himself into his chair, he leaned toward this sister in his church.

"Pastor Schroeder," she began, "I have to tell you something. Several things, actually."

Esther studied his face, a kindly face she looked on each Sunday as he took his turn to read from the Bible or preach in their congregation. Among the four farmer-ministers, she felt he was the one in whom she could confide.

"Pastor Schroeder, so many things—" Her voice faltered, her hand clutched at her collar.

"So many changes. You know our oldest son, Hermann, is in the Reichswehr (defense force). I know the Führer promises that the Reichswehr will only safeguard the German nation from the aggressors who would invade our country. But I remember the old days when Grandfather Froese told of the former ways of our church, according to the Ris Confession: 'Love your enemies.' Our young men, long ago, were objectors to war."

Pastor Gustav leaned forward, reaching out with a farmer's hand. "Sister Claassen, yes, yes. Our leaders clarify how we actually are for peace. Remember, Elder Bartel of our own village of Schönsee wrote in our church report, 'May God give to us, after years of war, a happy, honorable peace for the salvation and blessing of the whole world.'

"It is true. That old way of individually saying, 'I won't fight for my country,' is not held by the majority in our congregations now. When Herr Hitler saves Germany, it is understood that peace will come to the world. When we support Herr Hitler and Germany, we support peace."

Esther listened to the words. They were not new to her ears. Something was lacking. Somehow the ancient texts said it better. She would go over it again with Gerhard. Anyway, Herr Hitler promised no aggression, no invasions. Her son no doubt would be home again in no time at all.

Frau Schroeder set the pot of tea on the desk, filling two cups. "Sugar, Frau Claassen?"

"Yes, thank you, Myra. Reverend Schroeder, I am going to tell you something else that may shock you. Please try to understand." She sipped from the Dresden china cup. "Reverend Schroeder, we are keeping a Jewish girl in our home."

The silence hung in the air. Even the breeze ceased blowing the lace curtain behind Pastor Gustav Schroeder. His dark eyes widened. "A Jewish girl? Oh, my God!"

"Yes, Ruth Schwartzentruber who came to services and sat on the women's side with me is not a South German or Swiss Mennonite at all. She is a Jewish girl from Danzig."

Pastor Schroeder felt as if he had just been struck over the shoulder with a cedar post. "I shook her hand. Not a Mennonite girl? Why, you introduced her as 'Cousin Ruth Schwartzentruber from South Germany.' "

He sat back, obviously shaken. Without conscious awareness, his head quickly turned, eyes flashing a glance through the window. His long arm reached out, lowering the sash. He pulled down the green shade. After he had closed the door to his study, he sat, this time behind his desk. His large hands, fingers enmeshed, rested on his desk top.

"Esther, Esther Claassen. How, Esther, has this come about?" His eyes reflected worry and fear.

Esther told of their recent journey and how it had led to a dilemma which no doubt endangered the entire church community.

"Oh, my, Esther." Pastor Schroeder wrung his hands.

"What shall we do now?" A heaviness swept over him. Young men of the congregation going off to the army, the threats of war on the German border to the north. Now this—treason in his congregation and by stalwart church members at that.

He rose, pacing the floor. "We will try to find a way, a way for her to leave through the underground."

He had heard of such routes managed by persons whose names were kept secret. How could he find out more? Could they actually get a refugee north to the Baltic and across to Norway or Sweden? How?

"Gerhard says this will all be over soon." Esther rose; her lips had spilled the secret. The minister didn't dissolve in front of her. "Herr Schroeder, then we will keep up the act. When we come for services, we will bring the young Fräulein Ruth Schwartzentruber."

The pastor assented, becoming an accessory to the crime of treason against Herr Hitler's Third Reich. "She is Fräulein Ruth Schwartzentruber. Dark like the Schwartz- entrubers of Switzerland and South Germany, isn't she?"

"There is something else, Herr Schroeder. We have a new maid, Olga Fritzenheimer, who says she is a Lutheran. Nevertheless, she is an ardent Nazi party member. Most devout for the causes of Herr Hitler. She does her work well, but . . . I worry."

Esther's eyes lowered. "Herr Schroeder, sometimes I get the feeling that she keeps records on us, or that she may feel we are disloyal to the Fatherland. We are not, Herr Schroeder. But, yes, with Ruth we are, aren't we? Fräulein Olga may feel it her duty to turn us in. You see the plight we're in." Her voice faded.

Back in the little town of Schönsee, Chris Claassen parked his bicycle against the wall of the Baltic Sea Sun- dries Shop. He dug in his pocket for his coins for an ice- cream cone. Licking the cone in the warm July wind, he strode around the corner toward the Schönsee Greengrocery and the bank. Who knew, maybe Eric Kraus or Peter Koontz, classmates of his, were in town.

Suddenly Chris dropped his ice cream cone. It splashed on the cobblestones at his feet. His eyes widened in terror at the sight of the six swinging bodies twisting in the wind. There were ropes around their necks, and they were hung between the bank and the town hall. His young brain couldn't put it together. Herr Hitler would never allow this. He turned his back to the horrible sight.

When he turned to look again, his eyes moved from the swinging bodies to the sign above their heads: "This is what happens to traitors to the Fatherland."

Panting, crying with exhaustion, his young legs pumped the pedals of his bicycle. "Oh, Father, Father, how could it be?" Then he remembered—three of them were young soldiers in the Reichswehr uniform. The others? Old Eli Goetzke who lived by the river and sold odds and ends from his shanty. And the two Fellman brothers, Horst and Heinz, who were involved in some kind of boating or shipping on the Baltic.

11

Gerhard rubbed the leather harness with neat's-foot oil. It was better working with his hands than sitting in his den reviewing dairy records and management accounts of the farm.

How was he to deal with the boy, trying to be a man now at thirteen, yet with that wild terror in his eyes?

A month had gone by, yet Chris was still withdrawn. The Schönsee hangings foretold doom. It would be better if the boy talked about it and the other changes. Not all was good for Chris in his Hitler Youth program. Those long marches in the heat with forty-pound backpacks, ten to twelve miles a day.

"Too much stress on growing muscles and bones," he had told Esther in the kitchen as the young Chris lumbered up toward the veranda, hardly able to place one foot in front of another. Clearly he did not want to collapse on the lawn. A real man makes it all the way, doesn't he?

"Heinrich Wiens screamed in pain for three days after their last Jugend march. Anna told me that they finally had to take him in to the doctor at Tiegenhof. Flat feet. Doctor said the marches and strain were too much for growing boys. He will be in agony now and have flat feet the rest of his life." Esther had listened to Gerhard with a troubled look.

Gerhard didn't like to think about all the babies young German maidens were bearing for the Führer. Leagues of German young women were often encamped near the young Hitler Youth. A ribald song emerged, "In the fields and on the heath, I lose strength through joy."

There were too many things unspoken. Too often he and Esther had said to each other in private, "Better keep silent about that." Gerhard had to admit now that he too was afraid. He felt the same fear Ruth tried to hide daily, the fear that had not yet drained from Chris' face.

Then doubt set in. "How can we be good parents for our sons if we ourselves do not speak out?" They both thought it, said it to each other.

Gerhard doubted himself. "Maybe I'm weak. Maybe we men of the church could have organized. The Jehovah's Witnesses resisted the Führer's army, didn't they? Yet they disappeared into those camps. Is it true that some were shot? How is it in that land of the boiling pot of races and worldliness, the United States with its socialist president Roosevelt? Uncle Peter said, 'Mennonites, Quakers, and Brethren may choose an alternative to war.' "

It wasn't as if they hadn't addressed the issue. Their churches in their own section of the Werder had a conference over it.

"Scholar Mannhardt concluded that war waged against a nation with ungodly aims and decadent goals is a war in the will of God. We agree," said most of the clergy.

"But," challenged another, "remember Wilhelm Ewert, an elder near Thorn? He said, 'We belong to another kingdom, not of this world. We reject military service.' "

Reverend Ewert, with his proposals for evaluating a country's goals and deciding whether or not citizens gave in to propaganda to justify evil, hadn't made much of an impact. Ewert and his followers finally immigrated to Kansas, where they could put this into practice.

Maybe Reverend Ewert was right after all, Gerhard thought. He would have to listen more carefully to the Führer.

Gerhard had hoped young Chris wouldn't ask him about the Great War, when he himself was a soldier. How would he answer? But last week the question had come: "Father, did you carry a gun?"

"Yes, son, I carried a gun. I was in the infantry and was called on to help load shells in some of the great cannons."

His chest felt hollow as he admitted it. The half-buried memories now surfaced—the bloated corpses, the water-filled trenches, the shredded bodies hanging frozen in the barbed wire.

Then a worse question: "Father, did you kill anyone?"

How could he answer? Gerhard turned and faced Christian. "Yes, son. It was a war. I do not know of any war between nations where people do not die."

It was better, having told him. Better for Chris to know that soldiers and shiny boots and tailored uniforms pointed to something beyond—devastation, wailings, plunder, rape. The glory chants of victory were offset by the screams of the wounded and the gasps of the starving.

The barn door squeaked open. Chris stood there in his Jugend uniform, which Olga had starched and ironed to perfection. The swastika on the armband stood out starkly against its red backdrop.

"Good-bye, Father." Chris looked directly into Gerhard's fine dark eyes, softened by the lines at his temples. "Heil Hitler."

"Son, I'm proud of you." Gerhard could not speak of his love otherwise, the moment was too tenuous. Nevertheless, the love was known between them.

"I'll be back from our camp in four days, Father. Herr

Bowman promises nature studies, marching, campfire singing, and dancing with twenty of the League of German Maidens." The lad's eyes dropped and a blush crept high on his cheekbones. He was just beginning to understand some of Herr Hitler's meanings about *blood and soil*.

Chris hesitated. "Father, our Führer does speak for peace, doesn't he?"

"Son, Herr Hitler often mentions that the cause of Germany is to save her people in countries where they are persecuted and to bring only peace to our land."

Something bothered the lad. He dug the toe of his boot in the straw. "They teach us that the Jewish people are only animals with their greasy hair. You see the posters and the pictures of their noses."

He was about to say, "And, Father, you don't believe that, do you?" when the door swung wide as Olga Fritzenheimer called out, "Herr Christian Claassen! March. Promptness, loyalty, blood, and soil. Heil Hitler!"

Automatically Chris' arm shot forward. Clicking his heels, his adolescent voice cracking only slightly, he said, "Heil Hitler, Fräulein Fritzenheimer."

That night Gerhard and Esther leaned toward the radio. "Herr Hitler demands the return of our city, Danzig, and the right to build railroads and highways in the corridor separating East Prussia and the Reich."

What made matters worse was that Russia had just signed a nonaggression pact with Hitler. Who could trust an inferior Russian? Were they in bed with the Great Bear?

"You must respond to my demands!" The Führer commanded on the airways. But the Polish people had no time to respond by sending a representative to Berlin.

By the next morning, the German Wehrmacht (armed forces) roared across the Polish frontiers. One and one-half million men in trucks, tanks, and planes ripped through Poland in total war. Herr Hitler's warless war.

12

Because of her fever, Ruth tossed in the feather bed in Hermann's old room, still papered with deutsche marks.

"He that dwelleth in the secret place of the most High shall abide in the shadow of the Almighty."

In her half-dream state, the words of her father reading from the holy scroll in the synagogue bathed her aching heart. "Thou shalt not be afraid for the terror by night; nor for the arrow that flieth by day."

She lay in the fifth day of her fever. Christian had returned from his Jugend march with sweating brow, throat sore, and head splitting. Esther helped him undress and get into his own bed. Influenza swept through the Youth Camp and now here and there in the community.

When Ruth awakened more fully, her mind clearing, she looked out the window to the swaying trees. The trees. They stood in the fierce winds blowing in from the sea. They bent, they swayed. They did not break. She searched the sky. Today the sun spilled out from behind towering white clouds. But there were days when the sea mists overswept the land, and people groped along the country roads in the eerie silence brought on by the heavy fog.

Ruth's life was like that—groping along a lonely road of her life. And often there was the heavy fog.

The comfort of her father's words echoing in her heart now sustained her: "How shall we sing the Lord's song in a strange land? If I forget thee, O Jerusalem, let my right hand forget her cunning."

She would do it. She would sing the Lord's song here in this strange land of the Mennonites. It hadn't seemed so strange at all, that hymn these German people sang: "Holy God, We Praise Thy Name." The words, the harmony, the togetherness of it all sustained her as she opened her mouth and sang with the Mennonites in their meeting-house.

But several days later, when she and Esther loaded the spring wagon with a few packages from the store in Schönsee and headed for home, the songs had changed to mourning. It was as if someone reached into her very breast, grabbed her heart, and started to wring it.

"What is it? Such a train!" Ruth lost count of the cattle cars rocking and swaying on the tracks. Old Major reared slightly as Esther held the horse for the long train to pass before them.

"Oh, merciful Father." Esther barely breathed the words in shock. The cars were loaded—no, packed—with *people*, as the train headed eastward into Poland, now occupied by Germany. Glimpses of grimy, fear-ridden faces appeared in the slots and small windows of the swaying train.

The cars rocked past Esther and Ruth. An overwhelming stench drifted toward them. Now and then above the rattle of the wheels on the rails, they heard wailings. Juden. Jews. The sign above the engine proclaimed one dreadful word—*Auschwitz*.

It was a train of terror. Yes. Esther knew a little about

them. The concentration camps built by the Führer and Himmler were for the resettling of people who were out of work or disgruntled over something. Put them to work, good work in some kind of factory. All for the good of the Fatherland in its majestic effort toward peace for the whole world.

That was what she had read. But the fear that froze Ruth's heart now gripped Esther's. A cold sinister knowing seized her.

Ruth turned and threw back the blue cover. *Perhaps tomorrow I shall be strong enough to get up. Frau Claassen does so much for me. And Olga, too.* She reviewed it in her mind.

But there was another side to that—Olga. How did she fit into this family? Why, when Ruth thought of Olga, did she have to check herself? Otherwise she had a terrifying vision of herself running, running with a chill in her heart.

Only a month ago, when Esther stepped awkwardly from the back step, badly spraining her left ankle, Olga had rushed to her side.

"Frau Claassen! Oh, I know just what to do. In my own stint in *Bund Deutscher Mädel* (league of German maidens), I learned first aid."

In great pain, her ankle swelling fast, Esther felt herself lifted by the strong arms of her maid.

"Cold water, Frau Claassen. We must pack cold towels around your ankle."

Olga insisted that she stay on her back in her bed for three days, while Olga doctored the distressed ankle. Esther had had to laugh, even hold her sides, as the heavy Olga did a few ballet steps for her. Olga had put herself out bringing in a Hungarian goulash.

But those other comments: "You've been here now for three months, Ruth. Time to get you enrolled in the Bund Deutscher Mädel."

Esther always came to her rescue. "Give her time, Olga. So much to do here on the farm. It is summertime; let her have her music for awhile, then we'll see. We'll see."

Ruth knew Esther Claassen said that out of the burning hope that this all would stop. She hoped the Führer would say, "We've reclaimed our lands, we've saved our own German people. Now let us proceed in peace and prosperity."

But the Führer never said that. Instead he seemed angry. It was embarrassing, having to admit that he ranted and raved about the evil French, whose land he had overrun only a month ago. The great swastika now flew over the Eiffel Tower. Then Denmark, Norway, Holland, Belgium—all falling like dominoes in a row. The Black Spider against the field of red waved in the victories of Herr Hitler and his 136 divisions, the greatest army the world had ever known.

Everyone knew the hollow-chested British soldiers were like paper soldiers. How could they possibly have the German will and discipline? Or such commitment to their fatherland and to truth? The Germans read how the British soldiers and the French fled to Dunkirk.

Had it not been for hundreds, even thousands, of boats, ships, whaling vessels, and such, the war would have ended right there at the northeastern coast. Now the British weaklings had the gall to bomb Berlin.

The Führer and his splendid generals knew best. A few bombs in return over London, and the fog would clear. Britain would, as did France, see clearly the road to peace.

In the kitchen below, Olga was disgruntled.

"You show them too many favors, Frau Claassen. Forgive me if I seem too bold." She swished a spatula in the dishwater.

"How do you mean, Olga?" said Esther. Again that

pressure. *It's my house, isn't it,* she thought to herself.

"That old Beulah at the end of the lane. Our country is purified. Cleansed of Poles, Gypsies, and last of all the Jews. We've put up with their vileness, greed, and sloth too long. Germany has awakened and marches now in triumph, Frau Claassen. Surely you rejoice in such progress."

So that was it. Olga resented her kindnesses to old Beulah and her sympathy for the lonely girl in their midst. She tried to walk the tightrope and not show outright overprotection to Ruth. But under these conditions, how much longer could she keep Ruth's Jewishness hidden?

"Olga, is the chicken broth ready? I would like to take Ruth's meal up to her. She is stronger today. I'll sit with her while she has the toast and soup."

"The soup is ready, Frau Claassen." Olga slipped into her formal mode.

Esther brought out a silverplated tray and buttered the toast made from the fresh bread. A small vase of violets were reflected in the silver mirror of the tray.

Olga placed a napkin and a soup plate of steaming chicken soup on the tray. She nudged Esther with her solid, broad hip. "I'll take the tray, Frau Claassen. You need not take the stairs so many times a day." She said it with a downcast nod of her round head and with slight mock sympathy.

Barging into the sickroom, Olga gave no thought to the clatter as she set the tray down, carelessly spilling the yellow broth onto the napkin.

"Enough of this, Ruth. Why, Christian is up and about in the barn today. You were ill, that I'll say, but you weren't as sick as Herr Christian." There was disdain in her voice. She did not offer to help Ruth, who in her weakness was trying to pull herself up.

Maybe it was because of the fever still flushing her

cheeks, or that she so recently had emerged from her dream state. Anyway, Ruth was not aware that she momentarily slipped out of her Ruth Schwartzentruber role. Not until much later.

She reached out with her ivory hand to grasp the silver spoon. Dipping it into the golden chicken soup she said, "Oh, my mother used to make chicken soup for us. Every time we were ill with colds. But when we had the flu like I've had, she always made gefilte fish soup."

Olga, who had her hand on the window shade, turned to glare at the Jewish girl. The window shade snapped and rolled all the way to the top of the window.

13

It had taken Esther a full hour to get Olga calmed down. Lumbering down the stairs, slamming the door to the stairwell so hard the pressure blew back her kitchen curtains, Olga screamed, "Gefilte fish soup! Frau Claassen, gefilte fish soup. Juden! Juden! She asks for gefilte fish soup!"

Esther felt as if her whole body suddenly turned to stone. Now what?

Mercy prevailed as God gave her both insight and strength for the hour. With commanding steps, when her legs unlocked from their fear, she strode over to the bristling, furious Olga.

Esther grabbed Olga by the broad shoulders and shoving her into the kitchen chair. "Sit." Her tone was commanding. This was her home. She directed its goings and comings. "Now listen, Olga. My aunt Lottie, a Mennonite woman of distinction, always buys *matzo* bread at Easter time. She brings over some gefilte fish sometimes too. And Hermann always liked the pickled herring. Why, I might even have a jar of gefilte fish somewhere in the pantry. We can make Ruth that soup."

But Olga, braced on the chair somewhere beneath her

ponderous body, fumed. Her eyes glared through narrow slits. "You'll not be stinking up your pots with swine Jewish food while I'm in command of the kitchen, Frau Claassen. Not at all. I told you Frau Goossen also wished to contract me."

That was it. Throw in a threat. Get the old Mennonite woman with the reddish hair befuddled. Keep her there. Something as stinking as gefilte fish was here and she had known it ever since that evening and the Mendelssohn concert, when she'd had to take command for the Führer.

There were other questions too from the enraged Olga. Esther brushed them aside. Her commands continued. "Olga, you make the best sauerbraten. Come. Get out the three-gallon crock, the vinegar, the spices. We're going to make sauerbraten and have Aunt Lottie and Uncle Elmer Froese over come Sunday. Oh, you'll be at Lutheran service, but you'll have helped immensely with your fine cooking ahead of time. Come now."

Olga slowly got off her chair. She did love praise. Her slit eyes opened. Roses crept back into her cheeks. "Well, Frau Claassen, can't be too careful. You understand things these days. All for the Fatherland."

But Olga tucked the episode beneath the edge of her memory, as if stuffing a dirty sock under the border of the throw rug. One thing for sure, she mustn't fail the Führer and shame the Fatherland.

The next day Ruth, clutching the rail, lowered herself step by step to join the family. By evening, and after a cup of Esther's strong tea, her strength began to return.

At the table, maid Olga bowed humbly. "Fräulein Ruth, so glad you are with us at the table again. I've buttered you a piece of fresh toast and brought in the marmalade you like so well."

Esther, glad for the calm, smiled faintly at Gerhard. She wouldn't show her worry about Gerhard here at the table.

The evil had been sufficient for the hour. Smile. Give courage and hope. Where on earth was the rolling pin?

Gerhard, though, was not even fully aware of the cloud creeping in over his mind, like the April fog drifting in from the Baltic Sea. The two letters from Hermann. Such a stalwart son. So obedient, so dutiful to the Fatherland.

Yet the increasing war. Now troops were advancing again in Russia on a variety of fronts. Gerhard thanked God that Hermann had been spared that tragic first winter —the deaths of splendid German young men and the disappointing General's retreat. He had no doubt that victory was just a month or so ahead, and Hermann would again be here comforting them at the table, flashing his handsome smile, bringing presents for the women.

Christian, too. Now fourteen, how like a man he was. Yesterday Gerhard watched him stroke his face before his bureau mirror, checking the growth of the down on his upper lip. The boy would be a man soon, splashing on aftershave, courting, dancing. And he blushed as he talked about Greta Wiens of the Deutscher Mädel. How his face reddened as Gerhard caught him singing, "In the fields and on the heath, I lose strength through joy." The times were different, weren't they?

14

"I do feel at home at the services when we sing together," said Ruth, sipping from the crystal goblet. She would liked to have shared how her father might have reacted to singing "A Mighty Fortress Is Our God."

Jewish, yes. But not sectarian. He himself had read the New Testament. He always said that the things the dear Jesus taught were all in the Old Testament. After all, his parting words included, "Remember, Ruth, Jesus was a Jew."

Aunt Lottie and Uncle Henry smiled and ate the mashed potatoes and the sauerbraten Olga had taken the honor for fixing. My, how she had worked on it, soaking it in the vinegar and spices, turning it every four hours. Even the Führer himself couldn't be served better.

They all smacked their lips as the heavy platter was passed around the table. There had been ample left over for a generous meal come Monday.

"More fresh peas with onions, Herr Christian?" Olga fawned. She knew some handsome men herself, blond and Aryan like Chris, in Tiegenhof. Older, to be sure.

Gerhard had hardly said a word yesterday at the Sabbath meal or today. Esther didn't want to mention it to him, but with his depression lately, he had been spending a considerable amount of time with Herr Meckelburger and Herr Tilitzke at the Berliner Bear Stein.

Not that she minded that so much. Beer and wine were part of German culture. Friendly get-togethers around a table. A few pretzels. But the sadness crept from his eyes down over the lined face she loved so much. He had been like this when he came home from the Great War. They had had to put off their wedding for three months before his sadness lifted and he smiled again.

Well, it all would soon be over. The headline this very day was "The Führer's Peace at Hand." It was true, the Japanese had joined with their noble forces. They were forced to attack the helter-skelter Americans at Pearl Harbor.

But the Führer had clarified that President Roosevelt and the American millionaire Jews started this second world war. "President Roosevelt is a gangster," said Hitler. "We will blitz south Russia and win the war," he exclaimed with his usual raised fist. "We'll take care of America in time."

Olga had been quieter too since the day of the gefilte fish when Esther had commanded her to sit on that chair. It had made a difference, too. Actually, Esther wouldn't have to be paying wages to Olga anymore. Many German women nowadays had a Polish or French servant working without pay. Weren't they people now in debt to the rescuing Führer?

Then the phone rang. "How kind of him," said Esther, taking off her blue-striped apron. "That was Postmaster Brucks over at the village. Said there's a package for me. Probably something Hermann is sending from Russia."

Gerhard agreed; his face, sad all morning, lit up. He had better hook up old Major to the buggy so Esther could hurry over and get the package. With all the people coming through Tiegenhof and Schönsee these days, it was better to go in the brightness of the afternoon.

"Frau Claassen," Olga dipped her head demurely, "I'm wondering if you could do me a favor? I'm thinking of getting some of that fine Brussels lace from Frau Bergmann's shop, there on the side street in Schoensee, for my mother. Could I possibly ask you to bring me three meters?" Olga dipped her fat head imploringly.

Of course, Esther agreed. Then there was a grocery list, as Olga planned to try that new Hungarian recipe. She needed paprika, cloves, and more garlic.

Esther tied Major's halter strap to the post by the greengrocer. Katie Kroeker and Andrea Bergmann from her church hurried down the walk to her. "Oh, Esther, good news. Our son Adolf is to be married," cried Katie.

So they sat under the mulberry tree on that red bench, sharing the family news. Andrea, though, with her husband, Horst, had to put this announcement in the paper only three months ago: Herr Horst and Frau Bergmann announce, "For Fatherland and Führer, our beloved son, Matthias. Died in battle near Stalingrad."

It was an announcement Esther and Gerhard prayed they would never have to make.

How good it was—three sisters of the church sitting and chatting. They hadn't done enough of it lately. With the war continuing as it did, they were too busy holding things in their own households together.

They saved onions for that new bomb, and made balls of tinfoil for—well, Esther forgot just what for. Olga took care of that. And there were the French prisoners of war on their farms. Pierre and Jacques, with their funny berets, worked under the supervision of Gerhard and Esther's hired man. This gave old Beulah someone to cook for while she awaited Otto's return.

Then too, some of their neighbors were taking on groups of tattered and vermin-infested women from that concentration camp called Stutthof, fifteen miles or so to the north. Esther wanted to find out more about that. The camp director farmed them out to help with the sugar beet harvest.

"Oh, look at the time. I still need to go to the Linen and Lace Shop for Olga. Haven't picked up my mail yet either." Esther gave her neighbors a friendly pat and strode briskly over toward the lace shop.

She ducked her head as a ray of sunshine flashed in her eyes.

"Excuse me, lady." The voice was well-modulated, kindly.

Looking up, Esther saw that she had almost bumped into a clergyman, one in a black suit, like a priest.

"Oh, I do beg your pardon, Father—Reverend—"

"Howard Olson, pastor of St. Matthew Lutheran Church, Frau—"

"Claassen, Esther Claassen. We live on the farm a mile south and a quarter-mile east of Schönsee, Reverend."

"Oh yes, Frau Claassen. I know your husband, Gerhard. He brought those boys' toys for our Christmas collection for the orphanage. So glad to meet you."

Then it occurred to her. It would be friendly to inquire how Olga appreciated the Lutheran services.

"Reverend Olson, if I may inquire, our maid, Olga Fritzenheimer, attends your services on Sundays. You no doubt by now know her well?"

Reverend Olson stopped momentarily. "Fritzenheimer? We have a Jacob Fritzenheimer, a widower of the village. No, Frau Claassen, I have never met an Olga Fritzenheimer. Small as the village is, I would know her if she came to services even once."

"She's a rather large woman, Reverend, about twenty-nine years of age." Lines spread on Esther's forehead as she gave it another try.

"Sorry, Frau Claassen. I would know her if she attended St. Matthew."

Had it not been for another red bench under a bench tree by the lace shop, Esther wondered if she'd have fallen to the cobblestones. Cold fear clutched her throat. Her chest heaved. Her hand trembled as it reached for her throat.

"Oh, my God!"

Back at the farm, Gerhard emerged slowly from his study. He had been unable even to follow the details of the breeding records of his registered Guernseys.

"A walk. Yes, a walk to the south end of the farm to check the walnut trees," he said to himself. Fresh air, sunshine. Feel better after a walk.

"Olga, I'll be back in an hour or so."

Bruno, tail wagging, smile on his face, joined Gerhard for a traipse to the swaying line of trees in the distance.

This was her chance, the day Olga had been waiting for.

"Ruth." Her voice was unctuous, her head demurely dipped toward the kitchen tiles.

"Ruth, I'm wondering if I could have you take a half-dozen fresh eggs and a poppy seed cake down the lane to that dear old Beulah? She's so alone. Stay an hour or two. See if she's working on her embroidery."

Ruth put down her paring knife. She had finished cutting the carrots for the stewpan.

"Why, yes, Olga. Just a few steps down the lane. Poor Beulah."

Ruth sympathized with Beulah. Ruth also knew about disappearing people and the night terrors engulfing one when family or friends were whisked off into the unknown. Where had the Gestapo taken her dear mother and little brother, Aaron? Where was her father? He had assured her he would be safe. She would be with the Mennonites only a month or so. So far she had heard nothing. Only silence emptier than the snow-covered steppes of Siberia.

Ruth headed down the lane past the petunia bed, swinging a small woven basket. Meadowlarks sang from the side fence. Sunlight glistened from Beulah's whitewashed cottage ahead.

Ruth was at her best sharing with others. A smile touched her lips.

Olga dropped the edge of the curtain and hurried to the wall telephone. "Connect me with the office of the *Schutzstaffe* (SS, protective squad), please," she commanded. No time for hesitation. One doesn't falter for the Führer. No matter if it was a long-distance call to the Storm Trooper office in Tiegenhof.

"*Leutnant* Hockman?" Her heart thumped, waiting for the husky voice of the man who had been pleased enough with her to put his arm around her and pinch her waist last Sunday.

Old Beulah was pleased to get the fresh eggs. "Dear girl, I'll make a spot of tea. Going to cut the poppy seed cake right now. Sit. Have a piece with me. I get so lonely with Otto gone." Her voice faded with the sadness.

Beulah's simple cottage gleamed, though it smelled strongly of the boiling cabbage. "Olga tells me Otto'll be home any time. But, oh," she touched her breast with her rough hands, "oh, dear child, I wonder if Otto's still alive!" Beulah's tired eyes filled with tears.

"We must pray and hope, Frau Slavanski. My father always turned to the Psalms for encouragement. 'He will not suffer thy foot to be moved.' "

Beulah rocked in her unpainted rocker, allowing the

tears to flow. The child's visit was a touch of the balm of Gilead Father McCormick talked about at St. Anne's. She lifted her bleary eyes to her tiny picture of the sacred heart of Mary, holding the blessed Jesus baby.

She rose briskly at the singing of her kettle.

Such a tender girl. Why, Frau Claassen herself told Beulah only yesterday as they dug fresh onions, "Oh, I wish I had a daughter like Ruth." Ruth Schwartz—whatever her last name was. Looked Jewish, didn't she? Beulah had mentioned that to Frau Claassen, but she only pulled another onion and smiled.

Beulah opened her scarred wooden chest. She lifted out three fine woven pieces handed down through her grandmother's lineage. "From Krakow, the old days, the finest weaving." Her wrinkled, stained hands shook.

The ancient clock on the wall ticked a friendly backdrop for the conversation. When the clock struck five, Ruth rose from her brown chair. "Oh, Beulah, I forgot the time." How caught up she had been in sharing stories with Beulah.

Beulah lifted herself, her feet turning on their sides because of the corns. Leaning forward, she embraced the slender girl and kissed her dark cheek.

"Oh, don't forget to pray for Otto, dear child. Come again, come again. Give regards to Frau Claassen; she is so good and she works so hard."

Before Ruth took a step away from the chair, the sounds of a van echoed down the lane. There was no siren, but the vehicle was hurrying. The closed van turned into the lane. Dust flew from the wheels as it came to an abrupt halt. Out leaped two storm troopers.

Neither Beulah nor Ruth could utter a sound. Their eyes opened wider in pure terror. Their bodies went rigid as hardened cement as the door, splinters flying from the heavy blows, burst inward.

15

Only once before had Esther Claassen actually stood in her buggy, leaning forward, whip in hand as she raced over the dusty road homeward.

"Get up, Major!" The whip cracked as the tip grazed Major's rump. Wheels whirled. Dust flew. Terror clutched at Esther's mind. Her eyes searched for the roofline of her house.

"Ruth, Olga! My God."

Within her thumping heart, her prayer, a prayer embedded there for months, was becoming conscious. "Lord, save us from this hour. Deliver us from evil."

Ahead a van, dust billowing behind it, rolled toward them, careening from side to side. A wail pierced the air. The black-shirted driver and his partner raced toward the buggy, with its rattling cargo of wretched human beings caught in the web of the Black Spider.

Fearing that she'd be run over, Esther worked frantically to halt Major. She pulled the buggy to the side of a culvert as the rocking van pitched past.

"Merciful God above, deliver us from evil." But her prayer was lost in the wind, now turned chill.

Ahead she saw the whitewashed cottage by the elderberry bushes. Esther cracked her whip. White froth dripped from old Major's flanks as he leaned in for the last haul.

A disheveled old woman hobbled a few steps out from the bend in the lane into the middle of the road. Like a banshee shrieking in the sudden wind that sprang up, old Beulah wailed, arms flailing like a windmill. "Oh, God in heaven, mercy, mercy! Frau Claassen, they've taken our beloved Ruth. First Otto, now Ruth."

The old woman collapsed in a heap.

Esther jerked the reins, brought Major to a quick halt, and leaped out.

Olga Fritzenheimer ambled toward the dining room window and drew back the lace curtain. A smile spread over her face as she saw old Mennonite Esther Claassen trying to hold up that sorry old Polish Slavanski woman at the end of the lane. *People do have their problems*, she thought to herself. She checked to see if she had set the table.

The door burst open. *Let the farm woman howl*, thought Olga. *I have enough ammunition to blast them all away.*

"Olga Fritzenheimer!" Chin forward, back straight, Esther strode within four inches of Olga's broad nose.

"What did you do? Olga? What did you do?"

She didn't wait for an answer. She already knew.

Olga felt a tremor sweep up one leg, which surprised her. Frau Claassen was on a rampage.

"They came, Frau Claassen." She stepped back, but Esther kept pace, glaring at her sickly blue eyes.

"You traitor. You coward. We feed you, house you, pay your salary. You and your church on Sunday. Dipping your head at the mention of Luther's hymns. You Judas-in-a-skirt."

Esther didn't know she had it in her. But she knew she

was in a tangle of evil.

"Where have you been on your holy Sabbaths? I met Reverend Olson of the Lutheran Church today. He has *never* met you nor heard of you. I have a liar and betrayer in my house."

Esther knew she was now on quicksand. She had only hours before the rest of them met their fate through a Brownshirt.

She turned from Olga who stood there, a grin sliding sickly from her face, sweat drenching her forehead, just as Gerhard opened the kitchen door. "Gerhard, the Brownshirts have taken Ruth. We have failed the precious child."

Brown eyes sizing up the scene, Gerhard strode over. He put his arm around Esther, who was weeping openly.

What now? When trust in each other crumbled, when foundations tottered? Now what?

Face like a mask, he found his tongue, a tongue which moved with a deliberate slowness. "Olga Fritzenheimer, have you turned our beloved Jewish girl over to the Gestapo?"

"Yes. Yes, you have it right, Herr Claassen," Olga screamed. "Enemy of the Führer hidden here in your house." She emphasized the *your*.

Olga swelled with pride. Now it was her turn. "I smelled something rotten as Limburger cheese after you brought the Juden girl into this house. Pollute your own son Christian, a pure Aryan. Who do you think you are?" She lifted an arm, swinging it threateningly. It fell a few inches from a bloody butcher knife.

"Lax, careless, Herr Claassen. Vile books by that London on your son's bookshelf. Sidestepping the Führer's outline for our glorious country. It must end." She thought she would draw it all together, make sure they understood Nazi power properly enforced.

"Pack your bags, Olga Fritzenheimer. You're fired!"

Esther took another step toward Olga. The stones providing foundation for their lives, their home, their ways might be crumbling, but Esther Claassen planned on climbing on top of the brokenness. She would not let Olga bury her in threats and Nazi rubble.

Olga turned a fiery red. She hadn't figured on losing command. A loud, raucous laugh ascended. Her hand clutched the handle of the butcher knife. She waved it in Esther's face.

"I'll go, Esther Claassen. I'll go. Why should a daughter of the Führer reside with betrayers, pacifists, and Jew-lovers? I'll not spend another night with swine."

She brandished her knife, then stalked away to pack her bags. "And, I'll thank you, Gerhard Claassen," she said, forgetting about the titles Herr and Frau, "I'll thank you to stay out of my way. I shall carry my bags to Schönsee village myself. Why would I have poisonous traitors touch my things?"

She turned to Esther. "One more thing, Esther Claassen. I am dedicated to the Führer and to our thousand-year reign. I have Aryan men of my own. I am one of the thousands of pure Aryan German young women who long to bear sons for the Fatherland. How does that strike you? You and your purity, your strictness.

"Listen to this, Esther Claassen." She patted her broad belly. "I am already with child. A son for the Führer. What do you really think your lusty sons do with those maidens, and why do you think they sing, "In the fields and on the heath, I lose strength through joy"?

Olga's scornful laugh rose to the ceiling. No matter, lugging a few bundles down the road to Schönsee. Why, there were real men, virile men, Aryan ones at that, just waiting for her to call from the village telephone. Where did the Claassens think she had been spending the Sabbath anyway?

16

For five hours Esther Claassen sat on the oak bench along the walls of the waiting room at the office of the Security Service. Inside, the chief SS officer sat pompously at his broad desk, stolen from a former attorney who refused to bow his neck to the Nazis.

Esther Claassen made no plans to flee. There was no place to flee with the SS Blackshirts, the storm trooper Brownshirts, and the Gestapo (secret state police), both open and hidden, woven throughout the fabric of Germany.

Her back ached. Her legs and feet were numb. But strangely, a calm rested over her. And it was a Lutheran hymn that coursed through her mind, feeding her soul: "Were not the right man on our side, the man of God's own choosing. Dost ask who that may be? Christ Jesus, it is he."

No, Esther Claassen never recognized nor would confess to "the eternal nature of the will of Adolf Hitler, who endows one with wisdom of the Third Reich, and thus for all time." She saw the idolatry clearly.

Even amidst the tension and unknown of the waiting, remnants of her dream of two nights ago kept surfacing.

She had not known her Grandfather Penner well, as he died when she was a small child. But in her dream her grandfather's face appeared before her, white-bearded, smiling.

"You have a queen's name," he said. Again he said, with more intensity, "You have a queen's name, Esther." Then Grandfather Penner's smiling face disappeared. Three times the strange dream swept over her that night.

After breakfast next morning, Esther reread the book of Esther. It was true. Queen Esther. Esther Claassen had a queen's name.

And who was this Esther of old? She was the most beautiful of the wives of King Ahasuerus. She saved her dear Uncle Mordecai and all her people from the evil designs of Haman the Agagite, later hanged on the very gallows he had built for Mordecai.

Could it be that a purpose of her life, even though rudely hauled in by Nazis and faced with possible imprisonment or death, was to be a savior for her people? For Gerhard, for Christian, for Hermann's sake?

To her left, a hunched, thin farmer sat weeping, head in his hands. He had been snatched from his beet field. Blood from a recent beating had dried on the side of his face.

To her right a bulky, matronly woman towered above her, hair in disarray. She had a small bag with a few pitiful belongings, snatched as they yanked her from her bed in the early morning.

So far thirty-seven citizens had been taken by Brownshirts for their turns before the wide desk of the SS chief officer in the inner sanctum. In that room stood the five Secret Police, as spotless in their uniforms as newly ordained clergy.

A banner, fringed in gold, towered before them. Over it spread the dreaded Black Spider, multiplied several times on the dozens of flags around the room announcing the undebatable meaning of the hour.

Three of those awaiting interrogation, one a young man, tall but fair as young Christian, were shoved rudely down the hall. They disappeared behind the double doors to the holding cells.

Esther counted on her fingers each time a piercing shriek rose from beyond the door. "A bulwark, never failing," beat her heart, breathed her soul. So far she had numbered thirty-one chilling screams, not counting the thudding of truncheons bearing down on yielding flesh or the clankings of iron doors.

Yes, she was surprised that they hadn't loaded up Gerhard, too. But they didn't drive out beyond Schoensee without doing their research on the Claassen family. After Hitler interviewed a leading Mennonite of the Danzig area, he had said, "There ought to be more people like the Mennonites." The SS knew about Mennonites.

With young Hermann faithfully fighting in the Central Division, and Gerhard's record as a stalwart son of Germany during the Great War, they'd only snag the old hen by her leg, drag her in, ruffle her feathers, threaten her. And if she didn't cooperate, they'd stretch her neck by squeezing it between the bunk beds and wall of one of those concentration camps.

"Frau Esther Christina Claassen!" The voice of the shiny-booted SS officer echoed in the hall as if he commanded the very archangels.

But Esther was intercepted by a tall female, Sergeant Wilma Kloph. She was in the uniform of the Secret Police, hair wadded tightly in the back, her military cap shoved down and dividing her eyebrows.

"This way, Frau Claassen," ordered Sergeant Kloph. "You must be searched first."

After the early awakening before dawn, the rude jerking from her bed, the shove into the van, no water, not a bite in her stomach, a numbness reigned. Esther followed. It was as if "the bulwark never failing" kept her from fear. *You have a queen's name* flashed through her consciousness.

Officer Gerta Kittel shoved Esther into a narrow examining room for women suspects. One never knew what such a suspicious outback citizen might have concealed. The Führer's microphones and eyes were everywhere. There comes a time for stripping.

At first the floodlights blinded Esther, and the heat in the room was stifling. "Strip. Off with your clothes, Claassen!" There was no kindly "Frau Claassen."

Where had Esther heard that low-pitched female voice before?

"Strip. Now. Or we will help you."

When her eyes could focus, they fell on the heavy form of Olga Fritzenheimer, waving an electric cattle prod, bedecked in the uniform of the female assistant to the SS officer.

A chuckle reverberated from Olga's throat. "Surprised, aren't you, old lady Claassen? Surprised to see me here? Yes, I'm still with child. I'll bring birth to a glorious son for the Führer in a couple of months. Seeded by a tall and stalwart Aryan. The SS says anyone who distinguished herself the way I did by my services for the Führer—in the Bund Deutscher Mädel and in your home, Claassen, by turning in a swine Jew—could be promoted for this distinguished service. Strip." The devilish laugh ascended to the ceiling. She thrust her prod toward Esther. It sizzled on her hip.

It must have been the touch of grace descending from God above. For as Esther Claassen dropped her dress and lifted her feet to step out of her undergarments and shoes, her body and spirit parted. Not completely. It was if a silver cord still attached her to the trembling flesh far below her, as her spirit eyes looked on from above. Suddenly there was no fear. The mortal flesh below ceased its trembling and obeyed the hoots and raucous voices.

"Bend over."

At first the mind above did not hear the words or properly understand them. The human shoulders, breasts, and hips hung in space, faintly transparent in the brilliant light.

"I said, bend over." A shock convulsed the muscles of the hips below. The supporting knees trembled. The electric shock had only touched human flesh, not the spirit above.

"Spread, Claassen." The soul above witnessed the humiliations of a body below. But it was not itself brushed by such evil.

"Turn this way," Olga commanded.

Esther, mind so far above, was momentarily confused. The flesh halted.

"Fry her again with the cattle prod, Olga," sneered Sergeant Wilma. "She might croak one of Luther's hymns." Her devilish laugh rumbled in the room like the smirks of Satan's imps seeking the apertures of hell.

"Enough. Claassen. Put on your peasant dress and follow me," the brassy commands continued.

Jerking on her clothes, Esther rose, clutching the small leather bag she'd been allowed to fill with her brush and comb, a garment or two, and a coin purse before the Brownshirt with the long, ugly face shoved her out onto the veranda at four that morning.

She didn't feel the thirst, nor was she aware of any hunger, though she had not had food nor drink since the evening before. "The strangest peace overwhelmed me. It was as if my soul soared above my body," she would tell her grandchildren decades later.

"Stand, Frau Claassen." The chief SS officer, tired from the thirty-seven sentences he'd already delivered that day, squared his shoulders in his black suit. Glasses slipping over his thin nose, he stared at her.

"The charges against you are serious, Frau Claassen. Treason, by means of harboring a Jew. I understand our faithful officers for the Führer have properly removed the enemy of the Fatherland for protective custody. It is to your advantage, Frau Claassen, that you offered no resistance."

Well, yes. But that was because Esther Claassen hadn't been at home. She herself would have died rather than see the precious girl torn from the bosom of her home. She opened her mouth, then sucked back the words. Wait, something seemed to say.

"Do you have any witnesses, Frau Claassen?" The officer looked at her unctuously, knowing full well that there had been no time for her to secure a defense lawyer, and to think of a witness was ludicrous. Besides, who would have taken the case? Any lawyer who tried to defend her would have been thrown into a concentration camp. She was guilty, defenseless in this sham trial.

You have a queen's name. Again the words flashed across her mind.

"The Jewish girl, Ruth Rosenbaum, has been safely removed. No further threats to the Fatherland, Frau Claassen. But you are charged with treason for harboring this Jew. How do you plead?"

"She was a guest in my home. She was visiting from Danzig. Her father saved the lives of thousands of Germans, including soldiers of the Reich." Esther stood regally. She was surprised at the steadiness of her voice.

"Enough! You will not rationalize your evil against the Fatherland, Claassen. Another word of such rationalization, and I shall sentence you to Stutthof."

Agonized cries of newly arrived defendants rose from the outside hall. Thuds of nightsticks silenced the offenders beyond the door. Pain seared Esther's heart, *Oh, merciful Jesus.*

The war news had recently gone bad. The Führer himself was cranky, his henchmen nervous. The SS officer tapped his pencil on his notes before him. He would like to send a handsome woman like this Frau Claassen for some special duties for Herr Himmler's Kapos (camp guards) and supervisors at Stutthof Concentration Camp, he thought.

This time there were calls of "Stop! Stop!" then piercing wails, silenced by thudding blows against flesh outside the door. The waiting room was filling up. The commanding officer and his jewel-bedecked wife were planning to attend a benefit concert for the Führer tonight. He ought to finish this case, come down on some other cowering wretch who was obviously inferior. It sounded like such a one was just outside the door.

"Case dismissed, Frau Claassen." His mallet cracked on the oaken desk. "But, Frau Claassen, let this be a warning. I have before me the unexcelled records of your sons, Herr Hermann, who received the Crest in the Jugend, and Christian, who is a stalwart member—not to mention Herr Gerhard's being awarded by the Chancellor in the Great War for distinguished service. You will be taken for *protective custody*, Frau Claassen, if you decide to have any more *Jews* as your guests."

She walked past the pitiful wretches still huddling in the hall. She strode through the double door on her own strength, tall and stalwart.

When she saw Gerhard and Christian on the steps below, she allowed herself to fall into their arms. But only for a moment.

"Hurry, get out of this place. Who will be next?" She whispered from a pain-seared face.

17

It was whispered from inmate to inmate, though from slave to slave would express it more correctly, that Commandant von Gunden of Stutthof Concentration Camp never ordered his *Sonderkommandos* (slave undercommanders) to toss anyone alive into the five ovens behind the camp. The ugly brick towers rose in their shame, seeking to hide themselves in the gray mist and clouds sliding in from the Baltic Sea.

No, Commandant von Gunden made sure they had fallen dead from disease, starvation, dog attacks, or the electric fence, or that they had spent a few minutes in the gas chambers before they were received by the crematorium.

Ruth, though only sixteen, had insisted with blazing Jewish eyes that she was eighteen upon her "registration" at the loathsome camp, where daily the conditions worsened.

Unknown to the Jewish girl was the fact that Otto Andres, a Mennonite of the Vistula Delta region, first owned this very building where she stood receiving on her arm the tattoo—M 37689. Later, because of the town's strategic location, Nazis bought the building, a home for aged farmers. They added to it a hundred acres of land purchased from the county to establish their center of protective custody for Polish slaves, traitors, Gypsies, and, of course, vile Jewish girls such as Ruth Rosenbaum.

"You'll have special treatment," a Polish inmate, stinking like the bottom of the sewer, head shaven, whispered. "Young Jewish flesh like yours will surely warm Commandant von Gunden's hairy chest these damp nights. At least you may survive a little longer." The filthy woman, dressed in striped burlap, was hardly thicker at her waist than the handle of the broom she shoved feebly across the shining floors.

"Survive! Survive at any cost," urged Marga Stofskopf, a former Polish teacher snatched up for protective custody by the Führer's henchmen. "I will do anything to survive." Her scaly claw lifted the torn hem of her filthy dress, revealing a homemade knife strapped to her thigh.

But would Ruth? Ruth whose namesake was Ruth of the Bible? Did that Ruth do anything to survive? Were there boundaries she would not cross?

"Thou shalt not bear false witness against thy neighbor. Thou shalt not kill. Thou shalt have no other gods—" on and on the commandments rolled across her mind, as indelible on her soul as the tattooed numbers on her arm. *There are things I will not do*, she thought.

Ruth turned to Marga, who had befriended her after she had been shoved out of the tattoo line to find her barracks and place to sleep. It had been one rolling, billowing confusion, as if she had been caught in a revolving tunnel at the amusement park, then dumped on the shores of a land so ghastly it was indescribable.

Stench. Fog. Cold. Gaunt skeletons groping through the mud. Lice. Roaring blasts from the awful furnaces sending claws of flame groping above the fog on certain days. The smell of burning flesh and hair. Trenches behind the tar-paper covered barracks and rotting corpses, half-covered with lime. And the latrine—learning to hold oneself on the edge in the blasting winter wind, guts twisting in agony, hoping flesh would not fail, leaving the body to topple in.

On this particular October day, Ruth and two hundred inmates rolled the heavy, round sugar beets. Icy fingers frantically tried to get a grip on them and toss them in piles. Every half hour a bedraggled group of male prisoners, hunching in castoff coats, prison-stripe pajama bottoms whipping at knobby knees, halted before the mounds of beets to load them on the wagons.

The Gross-Werder cooperative farmers paid Colonel Van Gunden the pittance fee for the privilege of having Stutthof inmates duly occupied upon the fertile land—bringing the glorious cause of the Third Reich to its triumph.

Never mind that all around them the *Wehrmacht*, the German troops, were in retreat. "Blockheads! Traitors!" screamed Hitler when he learned that General Zhukov of the Red Army had forced the German retreat from Moscow. And even General Runstead in South Russia was turning tail out of the Rostov. Seven hundred miles eastward, British General Montgomery shoved General Rommel, the famous German Desert Fox, to retreat so many hundreds of miles eastward that it was a disgrace.

Nevertheless the Reich, built on lies, hung suspended in the air of propaganda and misplaced belief and faith before its final topple into the blood-soaked soil, burned cities and buried victims.

Ruth Rosenbaum grasped the beet, her bones rattling as she shook the heavy soil from it. She gasped as her thin arms miraculously gathered strength to heave it to the side pile.

"Don't let the guards see you falter." The words floated

back from Inge Worlitz, another Polish inmate who was snatched up for the same reason old lady Claassen got in trouble, harboring a Jew. But they were hated alike, Poles and Jews.

What did it matter? The Kapos (camp guards) leered at them back at the camp. The skull-and-crossbones insignia on their caps clarified the issue: "The only difference between a Pole and a Jew is that the Pole, being greasier, makes better soap."

The Kapos and field guards were calloused criminals released from the prisons by Herr Hitler's orders. Both Herr Himmler and Herr Hitler slapped their thighs in laughter at the brilliant idea. What better guards than hardened criminals? No bother about weak stomachs and soft consciences when it came to bullying prisoners, brandishing whips, and boning up on the other hundreds of methods of torture.

Already seven or eight of the older women had fallen in their tracks back at the edge of the beet field. Too bad they put on such a show. Who among the whip-wielding guards could understand that the half cup of slop the evening before, the two-inch square of bread (made of chaff and sawdust), plus that extra dab of lard was not enough to keep mortal flesh from falling on the freezing ground?

Both Ruth and Inge had long ago learned there was little they could do. The human soul can only take in so much pain and misery.

"Survive. Survive. Survive." The words resounded in Ruth's head. In her heart. In her very bending bones. The voice of her father. Where was he? His murmured blessings. His Shema Israels. Thank God the prayers of her father sustained her. She must survive to be reunited with her parents and brother.

Ruth knew she would fall if she didn't keep heaving the beets. Sink to the ground and a whip would finish her off, cutting the skin, breaking the fleshless bones below.

"You support the fallen, heal the sick, free the captives; You keep faith with those who sleep in the dust," she whispered, heaving another dirty beet.

"Draw a line. Draw a line," Inge kept telling her. "Never cross over. Death is better than yielding to their depravity."

When Colonel von Gunden handpicked Ruth to grace his quarters in the administration building, freeing her from the pigsty of the ordinary inmate housing, Ruth refused. "If you allow it, Colonel, I prefer to remain in the barracks. I am better suited for the work apportioned there."

She had dared say it and he hadn't knocked her down or turned the dogs on her. Instead he laughed. Colonel von Gunden had leaned back, shiny boots forward, leather crop in a gloved hand, white teeth flashing below his golden moustache as he howled in laughter.

"She dares to say no to me. Heil Hitler! Why most of the others would stampede to take up such an offer." Truly this was an unusual girl.

So far, no handpicked beauty had resisted his advances. This one wouldn't either after the treatment or after feasting her eyes on his table covered with thick slices of smoked meats, butter, and sparkling wines. They always gave in.

Ruth didn't remember all the treatment. God was gracious as she lost consciousness. She was up to her chin in the tub of icy water in the torturing compartments at the back of the main guardhouse, which squatted in front of the tall brick towers of the ovens.

Three times she had been subjected to the treatment. von Gunden surely believed it would soften both her will and spirit even as it chilled her flesh. But he would warm that up. His mirth almost overwhelmed him. "Salty little devil, isn't she?" He drooled, thinking of the warm youthful flesh. In time, in time.

Ruth preferred to die rather than warm the bed of an SS Colonel. But war's hilarity and insane order always throws in the unexpected. A sudden roar shook the roof, echoing through the barrack canyons. Loud "rat-a-tat-tat" of machine guns fractured the air. The guns strafed the inmates who ran in circles, some falling, some trampling on others, some running into the electric barbed wire.

"Not this? Surely not this. How could the Führer allow this?" Von Gunden was distracted as old Inge shoved her broom and pushed young Ruth out the door, where she cowered along the wall until the strafing stopped.

How could it have happened? Russian planes strafing one of Hitler's fine work camps with its up-to-date furnaces to eliminate corpses of the fallen and recalcitrant?

Why, only yesterday he had heard the war news himself—always, always, glorious triumph. How could it be? Weren't the stalwart Reich soldiers overtaking Russia, soon providing land for the eastward expansion of the Aryans, the true citizens of the world?

Von Gunden had been too preoccupied weighing gold pried from the jaws of the corpses lying in the front of the ovens. Too preoccupied with reviewing his ledgers and keeping carefully hidden his store of some of the finest paintings in the world and ancient statues imported from Rome and Greece. Too tipsy from the fine champagnes and full red wines purloined out of France. Too greedy for the finest of hams and sides of beef which hung in the Colonel's kitchen. Too filled with lust for Jewish maidens and their beauty.

Distracted by the Russian strafing, von Gunden failed to have the Kapo bring in this particular rebellious Jewish girl. Finally the Kapo dumped the unconscious girl at the door of her pigsty barrack.

Ruth owed her life to Inge and to Marga Stoskopf. Though they had hardly any flesh on their bones, they snatched Ruth up, put the half-frozen girl between them on the rough boards, and tried to find a spot with a little rotten straw beneath. They pressed their bodies against Ruth's icy flesh, rubbing her back, her arms, her legs, until their fatigued and thin fingers could no longer move.

By morning, mercifully, Ruth joined her fellow inmates in consciousness. She woke just in time to crawl out for the five-o'clock lineup, as the guards began the morning count.

"Survive. Survive. Survive." But for Ruth it was not survival at any cost.

Huddling inside the covered lorry on the journey to these fields, she had no firm knowledge of her location. Only a farm on the Werder, somewhere south, or was it east, of Stutthof?

Heaving one more beet with a groan, she heard the faint chimes. Turning slightly, her dark eyes focused on the tower of St. Matthew now visible as morning sea mist lifted.

Then the faint sound from the tower chimes. Oh, the blessing of the divine Father above, for it was from the Psalms. The melody wafted on the morning air. She remembered the verse from Psalm 139, "When I awake, I am still with Thee."

Still, still with thee, when purple morning breaketh,
When the bird waketh, and the shadows flee;
Fairer than morning, lovelier than daylight,
Dawns the sweet consciousness, I am with thee.

"The chimes of St. Matthew," she murmured. "Enough to sustain me this whole day."

Her eyes caught the horizon. That line of poplars. The

lay of the land. From this distance? Schönsee? The village of Schönsee?

The Mennonite church had no tower, no chimes, but the Lutheran church did. The church old Olga Fritzenheimer bragged about.

"What village is that?" Ruth pointed. Inge also leaned forward, trying to get her bearings.

"Schönsee. Yes. Schönsee. And yonder, clearing now, the very outlines of the city hall of Tiegenhof."

"Great God in heaven! I'm near my home with the Mennonites."

A whip cracked. She'd lingered in an upright position too long. A guard on horseback turned toward her row. Slaves must kneel and at least bend their backs like her namesake, Ruth, with those other women in Millet's *The Gleaners* scraping toward the ground.

To keep herself going and to avoid toppling in the earthen trough full of sugar beets, she made her brains review what she'd learned at the home of the Claassens. Dear Esther. Surely Esther was imprisoned for harboring her. And bright-eyed Christian, dedicated to his Hitler Youth activities. Where was he? Was his young flesh rotting in a shell hole near a battlefield?

And Olga? Where was she? Nazi of the Nazis. Ruth had known it the moment her dark eyes glanced at Olga's cabbage head with its little cold eyes. The smile spreading over her slick lips, opening now and then to shoot out words at whoever needed correction. Ruth needed no one to tell her it was Olga Fritzenheimer who had betrayed her.

Nevertheless, what had she learned among the Mennonites of the Werder? She had read her encyclopedia about them. The article said, "These are people who subscribe to peace and to pacifism with a noble history as people of peace for centuries."

How was it that though this was written of them, she knew not one, though there may have been a few, who dared resist the call of the Führer to don the uniform of the Reich? Of course, they would have been shot or ended up in the camps like the Jehovah's Witnesses. Were any Mennonites in the camps? Only time could answer her question.

But then look at her own people. They were often hated. Many were rich and most prosperous. They had the highest achievements—culture and music—in every field. Jewish teachers too, such as Maimonides, had preached peace. It was no secret to Ruth that many of her people chose to huddle over their lands, their estates, their riches, rather than give up earthly possessions to flee for their very lives. Why judge the Mennonites or Catholics or Lutherans too harshly? They had tried to shelter her. Many Jewish young men marched for the Führer though, because of their non-Aryan status, they could never be officers.

A whistle pierced the air. The prisoners dropped like lead weights on the hard clods. It was scientific, calculated by the best of the scientists and nutritionists. They had calculated and weighed and measured and tested in the camps. How few ounces of sawdust bread, how few spoons of watery gruel could sustain life in those bags of skin on bones. They needed to keep the prisoners robot-like, on the assembly lines for the Führer and Herr Himmler until the day they dropped and were swept aside as chaff for the fires.

And when the balance point came, that point when flesh failed, science concluded it was better to let mortal flesh sink to the earth in death. Let the bones and skin feed the flames; their supply of prisoner-workers from Holland, France, the Balkans, Poland, and Russia was as endless as the cord wood from Siberia. Soon the Aryans would rule the world. The supply of subservients seemed inexhaustible.

That evening when they were shoved by the guards from the lorries back at the Camp of Blasphemy, three corpses and seven unconscious women were tossed on a heap in the deepening twilight.

"Kapos!" the guards commanded. "Carts for Block C."

Beggars in striped rags shuffled out—glad for wheelbarrows to lean on. Glazed eyes and gaunt, soiled faces reflected no change of expression. All was the same at Stutthof—up or down, life or death, filth or spotlessness—the same. The inmates were soon rendered nonexistent when the death's-head battalion tossed their bodies into the heated ovens and the ashes dumped into the Vistula. The floodwaters left the sediment of the bodies on the Gross-Werder and the lands of the Mennonites, Lutherans, and Catholics.

In the spring, when seeds were found and sown, green newness would emerge from the ground—potatoes, beets, and the inevitable cabbages of the Fatherland.

18

Esther glanced out the kitchen window as she finished scouring the cake pan. Without even thinking, she nervously turned to look over her right shoulder. With her on guard here at the bottom of the steps, watching both the door and the window, Gerhard could have a little more security upstairs. He was up there hunched over his small shortwave, hoping to pick up news of the war over the British Broadcasting System.

And if he heard news, would he tell her? His face was leaner now, his eyes larger. He looked uncertain and weary. What worried her most was his silence.

Now that she thought of it, they had mostly been silent about the war and the Third Reich. Their souls were like streams in the desert, fearing the drying winds, sinking beneath the sands to preserve themselves.

Guilt rose like bile in her throat. What had she done, keeping her lips sealed in times like these? And the other sisters of the church, of the village. What matter whether they were Mennonite, Catholic, or Lutheran? Silence. Sons were scooped into the Reichswehr, donning blue uniforms of the Luftwaffe (air force). Even their own daughters were advancing into Hitler's ranks.

Why hadn't she spoken out? Yes. They belonged to a church where men and women kept their places; women were mostly silent in the church. But what about her namesake, Esther of old? She dared to stand tall before the king.

The last she knew her valiant son Hermann was in the air force, caught up in battles somewhere in Russia—in winter.

By now Esther admitted to herself that she did not trust the war news coming from Goebbel's state-controlled radio waves. Always, always, they reported, "The glorious Reich is advancing to bring living space for the German people."

She dried the pan, hanging it on its hook. Self-doubt flooded her soul. Why hadn't she been more assertive in the church community? Why hadn't the women themselves rebelled? Already now there were thirteen names of young men on that list in the church vestibule which announced chillingly, "For Führer and Fatherland." Surely there must be over three hundred of their young men now slaughtered on battlefields, shot down in planes or blasted in trenches.

Surely Ruth Rosenbaum was dead by now. The trains for Auschwitz kept rolling through their land. When caught at the crossing, Esther could no longer look at the cattle cars reeking with such piteous human cargo.

"God in heaven, save Ruth. Save Hermann. Save Christian."

She could see it in his eyes now. The fear. Well, maybe a mixture of pride and fear. He was almost as tall as his father now and in a month would be sixteen.

"Mother," he said, as his bright blue eyes lifted to her face, "the Führer is announcing a battalion for youth my age, the Wehrwolf Corps." Even the name of the corps sickened her. Werewolves. Animals of blood and terror.

God in heaven. How far they had fallen! And she had seen the light in his eyes. The Black Spider was drawing her son closer, closer, inevitably into the web.

She grabbed her chest, as the thought of the consummation crossed her mind. The Spider swallowed all. Then the Spider itself withered in the flames of war begun by the lies, deceit, and denials of its own foul mind.

In just two weeks, Gerhard received his summons. The desperate Third Reich and the by-now-crazed Führer summoned every available man from ages sixteen to sixty. It was unthinkable. Yet it was true.

Oh, God. And if she searched her heart, she knew she would have to admit that there were leaders in her own church and farm community who were official members of the Nazi party. "Herr Hitler made markets for our produce," they said. "Never have we had it so well."

"The Hitler Youth programs give our children and youth wonderful training exercises and help them develop their minds and skills," said Elizabeth Koontz. "Nobody in the church community ever did so much."

But Elizabeth was blinded. So were they all, in their own way, thought Esther. She thought of the story of the frog in a pan of water on the stove. Slowly the water heated until, without knowing it, the frog was boiled. That was what was happening to all in Germany.

What could Esther do to save her husband? "Don't go, Gerhard. Don't respond. We'll find a way. We hid Ruth for a while. I'll find some way to hide you. Maybe we can flee." Esther's eyes glazed in pain and unknowing.

"It will soon be over, Esther. On the shortwave, they say the Reichswehr falters." Gerhard bent over the back of the chair to cough.

"You served your time in 1917, Gerhard. No. No. No." Esther wrung her apron in her hands, tears streaming down her face.

"It is my duty. Oscar Goering, Heinrich Froese, Ernst Loepp—all my group at church will respond. No. Esther, I must go. After all, it is obedience to the powers that rule over us." Gerhard folded his handsome hands in his lap, well trimmed-thumbs searching for the forefingers.

She knew the doubt in his eyes, the touch of fear in his faltering voice. The same fear and doubt seared her own heart.

Never did Esther see such drawn faces and sad eyes as those of Sarah Loepp, Mary Froese, and Marta Goering. They leaned forward beneath the Schönsee sign on the platform as the train, loaded with the men, all in their fifties, shook and rolled on its way to Tiegenhof.

As the train rounded a bend, black smoke drifted back while an equally black cloud momentarily hid the sun. The smell of the belching coal and the gloomy winter landscape of the Werder was mirrored in the women's hearts. Was there any hope to be found beneath their confusion and grief?

But the teenaged young men—Christian Claassen, Ernst Froese, and Martin Loepp—lean and gaunt in their adolescence, tried to stand stalwart and tall for the Führer, and for the Hitler Youth Brigade. This they attempted even though the bloodred and black of the Spider on the sagging cloth on the pole drooped in the dampness and cold. The train wailed as it rounded the bend; the lamentation drowned their adolescent voices as they croaked, "Heil Hitler," with their gloveless hands extended.

19

Hermann Claassen's clean-cut face gleamed above the collar of his sky blue Luftwaffe uniform. Medals on his chest glistened in the light glancing off the windshield of his fighter plane.

It was easier here, over Libya, guarding the Panzer units below. Surely the wise Führer knew what he was doing after all. How could the unorganized, bumbling Allies ever come together on such a wide front? Italy, Greece, North Africa?

Hermann hadn't forgotten Operation Barbarossa and the terrible Russian ordeal. No. It would be a part of him forever. Why hadn't the Führer's leading generals given him better advice? Wasn't the Führer a military genius? But the pain and horror of his stint on the central plains of Russia lurked in his breast.

Andrew Brucks, from back home below Tiegenhof, had guided the fighter plane while Hermann manned the guns.

Below had been the German tanks, fanned out in formation, advancing for the Reich. All the fighters had to do was fill in the gaps between the tanks.

"Easy as old Tillie swatting horseflies with her tail," pilot Brucks had chuckled. Hermann, proud of his training, had certainly agreed.

But suddenly a Russian fighter plane had appeared from above, its deadly fire striking their fuselage. Flames had erupted as the plane fell drunkenly to the frozen earth.

How had the generals so badly miscalculated the awful winter which wreaked havoc on men and equipment?

With the Russians striking by air and on land, stalwart young German soldiers had grabbed their bayonetted guns and struggled over the frozen ground in hand-to-hand combat. But the military trainers of the Third Reich had failed to train them in hand-to-hand combat, and the dedicated Russian soldiers had slashed and pierced until the Germans had to surrender.

Now, knowing that his shoulder would heal after all so he could use his arm, Hermann reviewed that battle in his mind.

The young comrades, freezing, dying, gasping, had whispered to each other their doubts. "Are we being betrayed by the Führer and his grand generals?"

But when he and Andrew were given their medals, they had been reassured by the raucous voice of the Führer exulting in his limited victories in South Russia, "Now I have their oil. On, onward to the Caspian Sea." It seemed that the Führer was in command after all.

Healed and ready to serve the Führer in the small constellation of planes flying over North Africa, Hermann Claassen and Andrew Brucks sallied forth again.

Here was sunshine, balmy air, freedom. The unorganized Allies below were making attempts to land. What matter—with their training, their speed, their guns, the German raids would bring victory. All would be cleared. God was on their side. The Black Spider consumed the bugs, the insect Allies careening like tumblebugs in manure. They would be home soon.

"We'll be home in springtime for mother's apple pie," chuckled Andrew, gunning his plane, gaining altitude, and attempting to put the memories of Operation Barbarossa behind him.

A nurse approached Hermann's cot, here in the makeshift hospital somewhere in this fated desert land, far from the greenness of the Werder and the smells of the fat of the land of the Mennonites.

"Water, young man. Doctor's orders. You're to drink more water." She was a tired, older nurse from Nuremberg. One of the old-fashioned kind who lorded it over her patients. Nevertheless, he was glad for the cold drink. He had not forgotten the desert, the searing sun.

Hermann and Andrew had flown between Sardinia and Sicily. But unfortunately the Allies had landed there. He, Andrew, and the other fighter pilots had laughed, shoving each other as they agreed, "Only a matter of days. Our fighter planes are the swiftest in the world. The air is clear, our sights are clear. We'll blast them out of the sand. Out of the Mediterranean."

Andrew had chuckled. "Hermann, by summer, you'll be eating sauerbraten at my mother's table, making eyes at my sister Gerta."

But it hadn't ended that way at all. As if they had flashed back to Operation Barbarossa, they found themselves again under attack from above as an American plane pounced, flack spreading toward them.

They had been wrong. They were no match for the Allied four-engine bombers coming from behind the clouds.

They downed only one before the smoke poured from their faltering engine, and they plummeted out of control to the desert floor. But once again they survived.

"Contempt. Contempt. I regard the fighter pilots who gave up with contempt." Goering screamed through his telegram to their commanders.

"Each of the participating units in today's disaster is to send one pilot to appear before court-martial on grounds of cowardice in face of the enemy," the crazed Goering ranted and raved.

Hermann took the glass from the nurse. He drank, thankful for clear water, even though it was lukewarm. And thankful for a nurse, even if she was middle-aged, homely and had a sour disposition.

He and Andrew had agreed that their troubles had come because the befuddled mixture of Allies had stupidly announced that they would stop their barbarous attacks on the Führer's troops only on the basis of unconditional surrender. Who would have dreamed such idiocy?

Maybe the Führer was right. That American Roosevelt was a Jew lover and a member of the Mafia after all.

So they had struggled on. This time a raid over Libya. The juices were flowing in their warm bodies and their eyes clear as they looked down the gun barrels. Andrew was at the helm of the plane.

"Indians behind you." The message crackled in Andrew's ears.

There were enemy fighter planes swooping yet a third time. Even though the handsome young fighters were commanding a Stuka, they were unable to escape the advancing plane.

Then Hermann felt the searing pain in his shoulder. Moments later it felt as if his whole leg had fallen off as he lost consciousness.

When he gained consciousness and Andrew dragged him from the wreck out onto the desert sand, Andrew's words scarcely registered. "I'm only slightly grazed, Hermann." Andrew gagged at the blood and gore of Hermann's shoulder and shredded leg.

"You'll need to rest here, my comrade. I'll go for help." Actually Andrew never expected to find help. He certainly didn't expect Hermann to live. No shade. Scalding sun. No water.

At first there remained a little coolness in the mid-morning breeze. But suddenly the sun turned into a furnace and the whole world began to glisten, reflecting the increasing heat.

Next the flies. Not ordinary flies. No shoo-away flies. These were desert, stick-to-it-at-any-cost flies. They buried themselves in his wounds, shoulder and thigh. At first Hermann thought he would go crazy. He screamed, he thrashed, he wiped with bloody hands, grinding the hot sand into his wounds.

The hordes descended. On his face, in his eyes, up his nose. He grabbed his handkerchief to cover his face from both the sun and flies. His bloody hands soiled the handkerchief, drawing in even more flies.

He gave up again, losing consciousness.

When he awakened, the sun lingered in the west, blazing like burnished brass. His throat was dry as withered leaves. His only thought was water, water.

"Plunk." Something landed near him. Blessed relief. "Andrew? Andrew?? Oh, water."

There was no response, only the drift of the hot sand. Hermann uncovered his face, wiped flies from his eyes, and stared at the vulture looking down on him with its ugly bare neck and hooked bill.

"Oh, God in heaven! Mercy!" He screamed the prayer.

He heard thumps. More vultures, encouraged by their

leader, landed around the flesh cooking and rotting before them. In time, they would savor their meal. And the way things were going, half-roasted too.

"God in heaven." He kept praying. Then Hermann remembered his pistol in the side pocket of his pants. Could he reach it, stretched out like he was? Could he move?

By turning, rolling, gritting his teeth to keep from screaming, he searched and felt the hot bulge of the pistol.

When he had it firmly in his left hand, he rolled toward the stinking vulture. Its beak was now open, red eyes on him, great black-and-white wings spread.

Afterward Hermann couldn't remember how he had the strength to pull the trigger. Somehow there was an explosion. Then through the white breast feathers of the leading beast came a trickle and then a burst of blood.

At that point he lost consciousness again.

Andrew visited him in the makeshift desert hospital where he had been taken by a Red Cross truck.

"Old buddy, I never expected you to make it. Dried blood everywhere. I never in my life saw such blisters. Shreds of skin and blood, hands torn. You were burnt like the brisket mother forgot in her oven one time. More flies than on Meckel Esau's manure pile back home."

He had surprised them. He'd made it. When they took a good look at his shoulder and leg, they agreed that he might not even have a limp. The merciful God had answered his prayer. Christian could take pride in his older brother. And his mother and father could be proud. And what about that Jewish beauty they were keeping? She would be older now.

When the Führer heard of his defeats in Russia, Italy, Greece, and North Africa, he danced and raved like Rumpelstiltskin. "Traitors. Surrounded by traitors!"

The crazed Führer, sinking in the hellhole of his own creation, was being abandoned by generals behaving like prairie chickens racing before a prairie fire. "Shoot them. Shoot the cowardly beggars. Betrayers!"

The wild insanity enshrouded him, as Eva Braun, the woman he'd soon marry in a pitiful ceremony, reached out to take his drooping hand. Adolph and Eva, Germany's "royalty," deluded themselves into believing they were civilization's and evolution's highest achievements; they turned to the darkness of their mole tunnel underground as the Russian bombs exploded and the tanks rumbled toward them.

"We will never surrender. Blow up the bridges, the powerhouses, the government buildings, the factories, the warehouses—"

But his rantings were no longer heard. His leaders organized themselves to bring the unthinkable disaster to an end. They'd try to save what they could.

20

Christian's mind was more than troubled. It was as if something was trying to be born in him. Like his fellow comrades, he had given himself with unconditional dedication to what Herr Kroeker, his present Jugend leader, had taught him. No country on earth had ever risen to such exalted heights as their Fatherland. No country had ever had a leader who could be compared to the very Christ himself. Right was right, wrong was wrong. No one clarified it better than the Führer.

The avalanche of change rolled down on him, as if had opened the great door to the barn loft, allowing the hay to fall beneath, smothering him, crushing the hens below.

The voices of his ancestors called to him. He couldn't put it into words; it was only half-conscious. He scarcely knew why he had crept up the back steps, then on up to the attic, feet advancing on steps hewn by a great-grandfather who had made sure the work of his hands would survive for generations.

What propels a youth to seek out his past? Why was it that on this particular day something within awakened? A part of his soul was searching. Would he find anything here?

Christian had seen the book before. His mother, Esther, had read from it once. She had been cleaning this very attic and gathered a few ancient books, their bindings worn leather, and placed them in this trunk.

The Ris Confession of Faith of the Mennonites. He was thankful it was in German. He could not understand nor read the Dutch.

Christian knew enough of what was happening around him to doubt. And the doubt grew daily. Already the Russians were advancing through Poland. Chaos had erupted. German refugees who had been resettled there by his own German leaders were now fleeing for their very lives from the Red Army.

Already the British, American, and French armies, under General Dwight D. Eisenhower, had invaded German-occupied France. Rumor had it they were advancing, advancing toward the sacred German soil.

How could it be? So opposite from their Jugend training. So contrary to the messages of the flying swastikas and giant standards that proclaimed the reign of a thousand years for the Third Reich. So contrary to his brother, Hermann—his brilliance, his shining blue uniform, his praise of the grand songs, speeches, and marches of Nürnberg.

And his father, Gerhard . . . on that troop train shamefully packed with old men. Sad-faced, hunch-shouldered, ordinary old farmers with gnarled hands and reddened cheeks. By now they seemed so used to war, as most of them had served in the Great War. They were bewildered, confused, and even worse, silent. Just when they should be trotting grandchildren on their knees or vacationing with their plump Frauen, they were packed in a train off to do battle for the Führer. What kind of Führer called on elderly fathers?

The book was small, falling to pieces in his hand. Obviously at one time it had been read and reread. It was marked, underlined. Someone had regarded it with a holy respect.

Christian had found it, article twenty-nine, "Defense by Force."

> Regarding revenge, and resisting our enemies with the sword, we believe and confess that the Lord Jesus has forbidden his disciples and followers all revenge and resistance, and has thereby commanded them not to "return evil for evil, nor railing for railing."

He couldn't describe it, the challenge of the moment. A warm glow began at the edges of his heart, and what had been there before, a cooler emptiness, was suddenly filled with this knowing. An acknowledgment of something he had always known, but the red and black of the swastika had flapped before his eyes, confusing him.

As Chris leaned forward to close the trunk, he saw a large book that stirred memories of his early childhood. It was *Martyrs Mirror*, a book of stories and engravings that portrayed courageous men and women in Mennonite history. Chris had listened as his mother had read the stories to Hermann.

He sat on a crate to read several of the stories. These people had lived out Christ's teaching!

Chris dared to bring both books below. Though he did not voice the words, he was afraid. Such dangerous teaching. Such radical difference from the incoming tide rolling over him since he was six years old. Surely such books were seditious. Surely these were much worse books than Jack London's *White Fang*, which had put Olga Fritzenheimer into a rage.

Esther, hair graying in front, attempting to hide her worries and appear in charge, was startled to see the sixteen-year-old standing there, old books in hand, yellow hair falling down over his blue eyes.

"Son. You startled me." A breeze from a slightly opened window caught the edge of her mauve skirt, showing how gaunt her tall form had become. Unconsciously her arm, thinner now, reached out for the long handle of the stewpot. Feeling its weight, she turned and rehung it.

"Mother, we never talk about this, do we? This page. This old book of our faith. How is it that no one reads it in church? How is it that when I was baptized, this was not explained to me? Does it really mean what it says, Mother? Jesus has forbidden his disciples all revenge and resistance, commanding them not to return evil for evil? And why do we no longer read the stories from *Martyrs Mirror?*"

"My son, we have been too silent for too long. Not only your father and I, but our ministers and deacons, our county and farm leaders, our government leaders."

Arm around his shoulder, she took the boy, nearly as tall as she, and guided him through the kitchen and out the door toward the path to the garden. There, facing the road, they could see if anyone was coming. The "German look" had silently overtaken them all.

Esther also could not put into words all of this episode of sudden insight which had come to her tanned and lean boy. But within her heart was a knowing of a truth, a way—no, a life—they had turned from years ago.

Grandfather Froese had known it. He had worried over it, seeing the holy doctrine of nonresistance dropped from their confession. What if he had seen ahead—the idolatry, the worship of a nation, the bowing and scraping at the feet of a man called Führer. Now it seemed that most of what he said was lies. But hadn't a part of her known it all along?

And her dream. Grandfather Penner's face and his

words, "Esther, you have a queen's name."

"Mother, if we follow this way, this truth that Jesus taught, what will happen to us?"

Esther knew that Chris already understood the answer. But now was the time for her to be like Esther, to stand up for her faith, her people, the faith of her people.

"Had we kept teaching and living that, my son, not only we Mennonites but all Christians—and Jews as well—I doubt we would now be consumed by war."

She looked out at the Gross-Werder, the lowlands their forebears reclaimed from the sea and the swamps. How fertile, how green waved the willows. How peacefully swung the blades of the giant windmills through the decades and centuries. Oh, what songs the windmills sang of their history, their sweat and tears, their music, their banqueting on the heavy-laden tables. But now they hung suspended in a silent shame, as if to cover their faces with moss-covered arms.

"My son," she looked straight into his blue eyes, "had we followed what you just read, we might have known another life and maybe even greater suffering. Maybe we would have been imprisoned, shot, or hanged like the people in *Martyrs Mirror*." Esther folded her thin hands, the long fingers now at peace, not searching for the rolling pin or the stewpot handle.

"But, Mother, they died with songs of praise on their lips."

"Yes, son. They died with songs of praise on their lips."

The rumbling in the northeast was strong now. By looking at the clouds, one could see that not all was cloud. Threatening pillars of smoke rose from where the shipyards lay. The dreaded hour had arrived. The Werder was under attack. Soon they themselves would hear the rumble of strange Russian tanks, unless the Führer's magic weapons—some kind of rocket and a new plane called a "jet"—brought about miracles.

Esther didn't mention it, but in their own way she and Gerhard had followed part of Christ's great teaching. Taking in Ruth Rosenbaum had violated the Führer's teachings, his wishes. But Chris knew that, even though they hadn't put it into words. Perhaps Chris understood that when truth is experienced, lived, even if falteringly, it needs no announcing.

Maybe that was why the Führer ranted. He was lying. The weaker the argument, the louder he raved.

"My son, look. It is not over. We do not even know what tomorrow morning holds for us. It is a time for us to remember what you have read, for us to turn to the blessed Lord almighty. We may not be able to save ourselves. But, Chris, we may have a chance to die with songs of praise on our lips."

The strength of a graying mother, tall and thin, a mother whose prayers were often silent, but sincere and deep, flowed out to the lad, his yellow hair rising in the wind of the Werder.

As they turned toward the house, past the raspberry bushes, bowing in a chill wind, they noticed a struggling group of beggarly travelers dragging along. Who could they be?

One stepped a little faster, lifted his head slightly, and began to wave feebly, as if he was on his last strength. "Esther, Christian, I'm home."

Running to the edge of the lane, as the sun sank behind a cloud, they opened their arms to Gerhard.

He collapsed. "No arms, no guns, no supplies. We had to turn back. It is over."

Esther's heart turned frigid. Her long fingers touched her trembling chin as on the eastern horizon bombs burst, shells careened, flames and black clouds reached up to close over the sky. "My God. Now what?"

21

In only a few days, the Russian armies, intoxicated with an overwhelming sense of victory, rolled across the Nogat River. The wind of the Werder caught up the cries of those overrun by the tanks or shot by the wayside. The shooting, plundering, and ravishing were indescribable.

"You cannot believe the horror." The withered, war-scarred man sank before them. Bones almost poked through his skin. His haunted eyes blinked and hid themselves, now and then, in the grime and the stubble on his face.

"I cannot stay. Rest. Overnight, Frau Claassen. Oh, if I could linger here with my people, the Mennonites."

When he lifted his face, it was clear that the atrocities of war he had witnessed would forever be indelible on his heart.

When Gerhard had approached the Military Registration Headquarters in Tiegenhof with the beggarly crew alongside him, they were all given the startling facts.

"It is over for the Führer on this front. We cannot advise you. All you can now do is to try to return to your homes, salvage what you can. We have to leave this post.

We can no longer defend our line. The enemy has passed through Elbing and troops are now crossing the Nogat."

It was on the return, past Schönsee, that the wretched form had crawled feebly from under a culvert.

"Brother. Brother." The words were a raspy whisper from the trembling troll hunched at the edge of the culvert. "You wouldn't happen to know any Mennonites, would you?"

"Oh, brother, that is my faith."

He had looked as pitiful as the man who had received the oil, the wine, and ministrations from the Samaritan. That was how Gerhard Claassen, bewildered and with his own health failing, had come to usher the Mennonite Russian refugee into his parlor.

"Cornelius Ewert is my name. From Chortitza, Russia. Our churches there are abandoned, burned. Oh, I cannot tell you of the sisters, the women. Oh, my God." Cornelius broke into sobs.

Yes, it was a miracle that Ewert survived. Over four hundred of his brothers from his Chortitza area were now on their way in prison trains to Siberian mines.

"We valued our German identity," Cornelius said. "It was because we were Germans that Herr Himmler praised us, saying that there should be more people like us. They tried, but the German Refugee Service couldn't move us out in time. To be German and to be in Russia and now in Poland is to be given over to the fires of hell."

"We will do what we can. By God's help, surely we will find a way." But Gerhard thought his words dropped to the floor like lead. If there was any faith at all in them, even that particle seemed fake and hollow. How could he lead his family? What would happen to Christian, to Esther? Where on earth was his gifted son Hermann?

"I came on further," Cornelius continued. "I slept in haystacks, swam rivers. Afraid to go to any house. I bypassed all the towns and villages, fearing capture by the Polish police. God in heaven! They nail them to the sides of the barn." Pure terror was in his eyes.

"In the Memel area near Tilsit in Poland, the Russian army went crazy. Tanks rolled over the fleeing refugees, crushing blood and bones into the earth. They were our people. They had no chance."

Esther leaned in the doorway between the kitchen and the living room. Her mind raced. What about Uncle Elmer and Aunt Lottie and Cousin Eula? Had they loaded wagons, hitched up horses, and headed this way? Surely they, the Claassens here in this beautiful valley, would not have to abandon their farms?

All kinds of rumors reached their ears. Who could believe such reports? Maybe the Allied forces and that General Eisenhower would end it suddenly. Oh, it would be difficult, maybe again a terrible depression like the one that followed the imposition of the Versailles treaty and set up the fated Weimar Republic. But they would have their home, wouldn't they?

Esther Claassen did not know that on that very February day, Uncle Elmer and Aunt Lottie were loading two wagons with shining pieces of furniture, old heirlooms, silver, and valuable paintings. They were rich, and the things of this world had taken hold of them.

But cousin Eula boldly proclaimed, "I'll only get you started, go part of the way. I'll stay. It can't be as bad as rumor has it—about the Russians, or the Poles for that matter. No. I know how to fire a gun. I really doubt if you need to do this." Her denial overwhelmed her.

Then with two wagons loaded heavily, pulled over the frozen earth by four Percherons to each wagon, they joined the trek toward the Vistula Bay. Thank God, it would be frozen hard.

"On to where the Nogat flows into the Vistula Bay," they had been told. Rumor had passed it along, and besides, none of them any longer believed the German officers of the Reich.

Horrors akin to those of hell awaited them along the roadsides and in the fields. Fuzzy-faced German youth hanging by their necks, swung in the swirling snowflakes. On their uniforms were wind-tattered, quickly penned placards reading, "They tried to flee from their duties."

Soon they were caught up in a caravan of other wagons, carts, and hordes of refugees seeking asylum and escape. The beat of their hearts whispered, "A ship, a ship. There will be a ship. What was its name? Toward Steegen." They rumbled on as fast as their draft horses could carry them.

In two days they reached the frozen inlet leading to the bay and the strip of land where ships lay anchored. Refugee ships? They'd take their chances.

If they took the land route across railroad tracks, along the beaten trails, they would be slowed. Maybe the strafing from Russian planes would end their lives.

They took counsel. No. Better to head the heavy-footed horses across the frozen inlet and bay. "Don't let the ships be too full," they prayed.

Looking back along the trail where the willows shrouded the edges of the frozen canals of the Werder, they saw some of the shiny furniture heaved overboard. What mattered became exceedingly clear—the lives of mothers, fathers, grandfathers, grandmothers, babies at the bosom.

"I can see the ships," called Raymond Rahn, holding the reins on the first wagon of Herr Froese's small train.

"Blessed God in heaven. We have arrived. And the ice is heavy, Folks here, according to the German officer waving us on, say that the ice is over three feet deep. We are saved." Raymond Rahn cracked the whip over the backs of Herr Froese's Percherons.

Uncle Elmer followed after as he held his reins and guided his four obedient Percherons down the slight incline out onto the snow-covered ice of the Vistula Bay.

It was true. Solid ice. Mother Froese wrapped the woolen muffler tighter on her throat as she called, "We'll be to our rescue in less than an hour." She fingered the locket and the strand of pearls hidden in her bosom.

Behind them, six more wagons descended onto the ice. The passengers had relieved faces and less pain in their hearts. There was no strafing, no serious tragedy. Their drivers were maneuvering them at last through the perils of "the arrow that flieth by day."

"I can see the smoke from the ships' stacks," cried Lottie.

Their joy near the end of their journey was overwhelming as some of them sang, "Holy God, we praise thy name: Lord of all, we bow before Thee; All on earth thy scepter claim, All in—"

But before the singers could mouth the words "heav'n above adore thee," there was a crack like that of a giant whip. Surely the drivers were not abusing the Percherons at the last hour?

Next a thunder. But thunder from below. As Aunt Lottie looked out to see what made such ear-shattering noise, the four Percherons and the wagon ahead of her disappeared in the blackest waters she had ever seen.

Lottie Froese only had time to turn and scream, "The ice, it is breaking," as the wagon in which she rode high dropped into the depths.

Then silence reigned. Silence, except for momentary clanking of the glistening edges of the jagged ice. Then they closed over the descending weights that had ruptured the frozen surface.

22

"Our people have been here since the middle of the sixteenth century." Gerhard turned the Delft blue cup, warming his hands. The last of the coffee Esther had made for him braced him momentarily. That was like Esther. Always giving the best or the last to someone else.

His mind wandered over the history of his people, the way they had salvaged the land from the sea, built their sturdy houses, their barns. From swampy wastelands to a veritable garden with their windmills, villages, churches, and the cobblestone streets of their villages. Everywhere red tile roofs contrasted against the blue of the sky. Homeland. A beloved homeland.

"I'll make a cup of tea for myself," Esther said, making every attempt to smile cheerfully. It was if the island were being torn by a giant hand grasping the fertile soil where the Vistula and Nogat separated, shaking them, as if to jar them from the earth.

"The whole land is breaking apart. What could not be has come about. My God! What are we to do?" She concentrated on getting Gerhard back on his feet. For seven days following his return, he had lain in his room, curtains pulled, tossing feverishly.

She and Christian struggled with the necessary chores. They milked the registered guernseys and cared for the brood sows. Blooded stock. Weren't their people noted for the breeding of the finest livestock?

Esther had heard the reports—but maybe they couldn't be believed—about families on the other side of the Nogat who had started to flee. Loading wagons, heading for the ports on the Vistula Bay. How could they leave their homes? The Führer had promised peace. No wars on German soil. How could it be?

Esther glanced at Gerhard who was wrapped in the sweater she had knitted from their own wool, with his feet on a footstool. She was thankful that the color was returning to his cheeks. How white his hair was turning.

And herself? She glanced at herself only briefly in the mirror. The streaks were there too in her hair. But her strength held, thank God. She hoped that the Werder would soon be left battle free, that the Russian troops would advance to the cities, to Danzig, then on into the heartland. In the cities there would be reveling, drinking, whatever excesses of the victors. But not here.

Christian, leaning on his toes, worried and confused, looked out the kitchen window. A February gloom settled over everything. A dirty van slowly rocked down the road. Few cars were seen now because of gasoline shortages. It had to be a military van. It turned into their lane, past old Beulah's cottage.

Poor old woman and her Catholic relics and her Polish prayers. Though she was a German citizen, her heart was Polish. She had given up any hope of seeing Otto again.

Chris answered the knock on the door. There was a hasty greeting as the older military deputy handed him the order: "All sixteen-year-olds report for the student *Flackhelfer* for Führer and Fatherland."

So at last the legs of the Black Spider encircled him. Flackhelfer was a unit of teenagers ordered to the trenches and ditches in a desperate attempt to ward off the impossible—ward it off with cast-off guns, helter-skelter armaments, grenades, and refurbished tools of war.

What can a mother do when her ears first hear such news? At first she felt only shock and disbelief. She sat, burgundy dress falling about her long thighs as she perched on the edge of the bent-willow chair. "No! Not Christian."

Then she realized that excessive outburst would only increase the sufferings of her son. Their recent talk, the faith statement that had gripped his adolescent heart, confirmed his growing faith. Even her hands were still, not searching for a kitchen utensil.

She stood, reached out with her mother's arms, full clothed in long sleeves. She embraced him tenderly with the arms of mother love, the arms of sacrifice, the arms of prayer.

"My son, I know God will sustain you. We cannot rely on our strength. Human strength is not enough. You must believe it."

How feeble her words sounded. How useless and futile. How little seemed her faith. But they were human words, prompted by a deeper anchoring. And words so grounded have, in their time, their own fulfillment. This Esther knew, even if hollowness and chill clutched at her bosom.

As he left with a small rucksack, she called after him. "My son, the medics, the medics. Ask them to allow you to work with the medics, to tend to the sick and wounded. It would be the way of the blessed Jesus."

Then her voice failed. She turned to Gerhard, standing behind her, and allowed herself the luxury of burying her face in his sweater as sobs overwhelmed her.

So Christian Claassen, tall and thin in his adolescence, strode off to the village of Schoensee where he was joined by Arthur Krahn and Peter Martens and a straggly group of other teenagers. Some shoved, laughed, pounded each other's backs as their young blood surged at the new stimulant—their identities as soldiers.

The fragments of hope in their hearts struggled to overcome the dark fears lurking beneath. They had been taught to be obedient to the Fatherland and to the voice of the Führer. How could their feet turn otherwise?

Esther leaned precariously on the wagon seat next to Gerhard. She had wanted to drive the team of Clydesdales, but Gerhard had reached for the reins, attempting to sit tall. He needed to be in charge, even though his cough racked his thinning frame.

Village sirens wailed, calling the villagers, calling the surrounding farmers. Some galloped in on horseback. Some arrived with legs aching from pedaling bicycles. Some walked awkwardly on feet with corns and bunions. They gathered in the square at Schönsee.

There a potbellied military adviser, representing the government of the Reich, finally commanded their attention. "Citizens of Deutschland, comrades of the Werder, the front of our noble army has broken. I report our officers and troops are in retreat." All military pomp and starch wilted from his body.

His announcement was unneeded. The rumbling of planes and Russian tanks was clearly audible.

"Your Reich government has set up a refugee plan. We urge you to flee with all speed toward the river bridge east of Schönsee, the great bridge that spans the Vistula. There you will find our noble German troops waiting to help you up the Vistula to the bay. Whaling vessels will carry you on to west Germany. The wishes of the Fatherland and the

Führer are with you. Heil Hitler."

How could he say it at this hour? Germany was crumbling, the beautiful cities of Dresden, Frankfurt, Regensberg, and Berlin were all bombed to rubble and ashes. But false promises, believed and loved, are hard to abandon. Denial that closes hearts and eyes comes easier.

A Russian bomber zoomed earthward as citizens ran helter-skelter for cover, fearing strafing on the square. East of the village black smoke from the craters of freshly dropped bombs swirled heavenward.

Flee, flee, flee, like the Israelites fleeing Egypt, hordes of Pharaoh's chariots behind them.

So the Mennonites, Lutherans, and Catholics poured out on the streets, the byways, the trails toward the Vistula. They pitched hastily snatched food and belongings, some foolishly thrown and dumped into wagons without thought.

Panic lay at the edge of every heart. Here and there the panic broke through in a scream or nervous wailing. Germans all. Loyal citizens who had tried to support the Third Reich, to obey, to do as they were told under the Spider on the red and white flag.

Esther breathed a prayer as Gerhard took the reins, slapping them on the rumps of Elzer and Mose. Then Esther heard a voice above the murmurings of the fleeing hordes. "Mother, Father, wait. Wait."

They turned together, the hunching man and the mother with the plaid kerchief protecting her ears from the bitter wind.

Christian leaned into the wind as he ran around the bend by the stark branches of the elderberry bushes at the corner of old Beulah's cottage. "Mother, Father, wait."

A strong young arm reached out. His hand grasped the front edge of the wagon as Gerhard brought the team to a halt.

"We were dismissed. The Russian tanks rumbled down the streets. Our leaders waved white sheets and flags. 'Home, go home, the military advisers yelled.' "

The pitching wagon stopped only long enough for Esther to leap out and grab her son, smothering him with her kisses, while hundreds of fellow refugees crowded past.

"Oh, Mother, now what do we do? Where are Grandfather and Grandmother Froese?"

"They are safe for now, son. Inside the wagon."

There they huddled, wrapped in blankets, hunched on the two hard chairs, abandoning the land of their birth, the land of their parents and parents' parents who had claimed the Werder from the sea.

On the other side of the wagon, beneath the canvas cover, sat old Polish Beulah, her grimy face almost as black as her torn and soiled garments, her black mouth reeking of boiled cabbage and garlic. She clutched her beads with equally grimy hands as she mouthed the words of the rosary, the hairs trembling on her chin.

Outside, Mennonite refugee Cornelius Ewert clutched a bridle as he murmured his own prayers and words of comfort to the nervous horses and the pilgrims and strangers, refugees all. He prayed he'd be able to escape showing papers; his papers had been taken by the Polish ragamuffin deputies now serving the Red Army on the other side of Schönsee.

23

The wagons, carts, wheelbarrows, and struggling refugees, backs bending, arms drooping with baggage, at last made some semblance of order between the fence rows, the barren ash trees, and the stands of willow at the edges of the drainage ditches.

They were quieter too, for part of the agony of being jerked from their homes was being tempered and buried by psychological powers unnameable to them. They joined the millions of others now homeless, many beggars and many wounded, blood seeping through their bandages.

Chris walked ahead of Mose and Elzer. He caught up with Arthur Krahn from his church. There they walked, two Mennonite youth caught between the intoxicating whirl of the events surrounding them and the denials covering the fears of their hearts.

"We'll make it," said Arthur, pulling the ear tabs on his cap down tighter to ward off the bitter wind. "My dad says this will be over in no time at all. He plans to be back for spring planting."

But Chris was of another mind. He had seen the white flags waving from offices, from the town hall, from beggarly groups of German soldiers. "In time. Maybe we will have to settle for awhile in Denmark or in west Germany. Herr Hitler took care of our own people from Chortitza and Molotschna, didn't he? We can count on the Fatherland. Herr Hitler only wanted living space, *Lebensraum*, for his dedicated people. My father says Herr Hitler financed land in Paraguay for his faithful Aryan people to resettle."

But even Chris was aware that he mouthed the words too loudly. And they were not convincing, not even registering in his own heart. It takes a day or two for stark reality to bare her skeletal forms.

Inside the wagon, Esther dug for a comforter. Rolling it, she shoved it between the wooden trunk and the aching backs of Grandmother and Grandfather Froese. Resignation reflected from their eyes. Grandfather Arnold, now eighty-two, turned a page of his worn Bible with trembling hand. He could not read the words because of the shaking of the wagon, but to hold the book and to turn its blessed pages comforted him. Beside him tiny Grandmother Marie shrank even smaller into the comforter Esther had placed around her. Her lips breathed the Lord's Prayer while, nestled on the other side, old Beulah counted her beads.

"Make way, to the side. Over, over!" Raucous voices rose above the belch and roar of an army truck, as the small convoy of German soldiers attempted to weave its way through the refugees without overrunning them.

Horns blared. Horses neighed in fright. Stragglers crowded each other toward the edges of the road by the deep drainage ditches, praying not to topple into the frigid waters below.

Toward evening, when the winter gloom finally overcast the sun, their hearts turned to despair. They began gathering in small groups.

"I told you not to bring that." Arguments broke out. Books, vases, clocks, garnishments of shelf and cupboard strained their backs, pulled at their shoulders until they had to hold back their screams.

"Throw it out. Dump that heavy crystal bowl. Oh, no! That belonged to Great-grandmother Celia."

Feelings worsened as the things of this world were abandoned in piles along the roadsides, soon to be snatched by a wanderer seduced by the glitter.

Elzer and Mose, as bewildered at their task as the freezing hordes along their sides, strained over the frozen ruts toward the town of Fürstenwerder. In another day, they'd be approaching the Vistula River and the bridge.

"Oh, merciful God," breathed Esther, now taking the reins as Gerhard started shivering with one of his chills. She had put him inside alongside the grandparents.

Soup, hot broth? How would she make it? Over what fire? Where? The reality of being refugees made its inroads on her. She reviewed in her mind the medicines she had snatched from the medicine chest. Aspirin, unfortunately too few, but no time to buy more. She had rolled them—the aspirin, a small bottle of Alpenkräuter (the alpine "cure-all" herbs), and a roll of bandages—into a shawl she bound around her waist.

As the twilight deepened, one deacon, Howard Mannhardt, waved his gloved hand. He turned to the cluster around the Claassen wagon. "Up ahead the ground is flat, and there is a woods. Trees not too thick. Maybe we can camp for the night. We need to get the elderly, women, and children settled. Build some fires and drag out some kettles."

It sounded so helplessly primitive, like vagabonds. Could it be true that such prosperous people, Aryans, some with fine china and sterling silver in their chests, the best of leather on their feet, had to travel like this?

But a little cluster of women from Esther's Mennonite church got to work, dragging out kettles, pots, pans, while older youth and husbands searched for dry fallen limbs to begin the fires. They ate chunks of the hams and shoulders stuffed among the snatched belongings. A huge kettle of soup, made with beans and chunks of smoked ham and sausages, sent out a heavenly aroma.

Deacon Mannhardt said a prayer for their group, among the fifty or so groups gathered here and there, each with its own emergency organization. All looked forward to day after tomorrow when again their noble soldiers under the Third Reich would take over, giving them directions, leading them across the Vistula. The soldiers would send them off to west Germany with the blessings of the best for the Reich. A dip in fortunes for all, yes, but another day another Reich would surely rise.

It was difficult and embarrassing for Chris and his buddy, Arthur Krahn, and other young males, but not as embarrassing and even shocking for Lorilee Rempel and Lila Epp, teenage girls from his own church, when they figured out what to do when the call of nature forced them to respond.

They quickly realized that privacy had to be left behind. Shame or no shame, their adolescent bodies were exposed now and then, accidentally, haphazardly, and by chance to other bewildered eyes. It was as if someone or something outside of them was painfully stripping away their identities, who they were as human beings. A mocking force, bloated by war, was unleashed to play havoc with their lives.

That first night didn't turn out so bad. Winter, yes. Cold, yes. But in the wagon beds, they burrowed under the mufflers, quilts, and comforters.

Snow fell on the second day. It blew in with gale force off the Baltic Sea, as they rumbled through Fürstenwerder, the hard cobblestones shaking the bones of the elderly inside the wagons.

Fürstenwerder, princely town of the Werder. Could it be? Houses were abandoned, doors and windows open. Helter-skelter vagabond groups of God-knew-what-kind of military personnel were rummaging through.

Hundreds of embattled Poles, in agreement with the Communist cause, now reveled in newfound companionship with the Russians, as the Red Army invited them to join in plundering and in drinking the vodkas and wines from the cellars of the villages.

Do not even mention the women and the children they ran across. Even the wind ceased howling at the shameful orgies.

24

Gerhard worried about his blooded Clydesdales, Mose and Elzer, now tied to the front of the wagon, stomping and blowing occasionally throughout the night. They had grazed the winter grasses around the clearing, sipped water from the melted snow and ice brought to them in buckets. So many unknowns. Surely he would not have to turn them loose?

But then, life for them all was open, frightening, with no real and discernible edges like they had been so used to for so long in the Third Reich. Then it had been clear. They had been obedient and there were no gray areas. The Black Spider represented the TRUTH akin to the very Christianity with which they had grown up.

What now with such crumbling beneath their souls and feet? Esther slept fitfully, crouched in an upright position between bags of potatoes and flour. Long past midnight, though, she slumbered, a fatiguing, uneasy slumber.

"You have a queen's name. You have a queen's name."

She was partially conscious, conscious enough to be aware that she was dreaming, awake enough to question whether she would be able to catch hold of the dream and ponder its meaning when dawn broke.

Somewhere a sick child cried and coughed above the sorrowful wind. And when dawn broke? What then? "Oh, God," she began to pray again. She prayed that she would open herself, like Esther of old, to the truth for her in the bottomless bog of the present journey.

Christian couldn't sleep until near daybreak. When he drifted off, a vision of a great flag, bloodred with a revolving circle, whirled and waved toward him like an angry serpent. The Black Spider grasped for a hold on the whirling center. Then a bulging head loomed from the middle of the Spider. Chris's young shoulders jerked, terror gripped his throat. He gurgled, muscles tightening, as two blood-streaked eyes protruded from the octopus head, imploring, seducing, entrapping, as a snake hypnotizes a bird on a branch before swallowing it.

The camp of refugees awakened in disarray. A covey of Russian planes flew low. They rumbled above the fog of the lowlands, which enshrouded the trees with a thick hoarfrost and turned them into silent ghosts reaching out to the homeless and frightened.

The ground jolted from heavy bombings and artillery fire. It was somewhere beyond, surely way beyond the Vistula and its great bridge.

In each group, some of hundreds, some of fifties, someone with inner strength took command. They were stumbling on their way again. If their feet faltered, they would soon be overrun by the hoards.

By ten o'clock the skies had cleared and the sun shone brightly against a cloudless blue. Now they were vulnerable to the bombing and the strafing from planes above.

Then to Gerhard's dismay, the frozen mud of the road beneath the Clydesdale's feet softened, as early February gave one of her hints of spring. The heavy wagons began to mire in the mud.

"Gee! Haw! Get on!" Whips cracked, riders descended, sinking fine leather shoes and boots in the increasingly soft mud. The horses strained and the men pushed.

Finally, the inevitable. They'd have to heave belongings from the wagons. The horses were wet with foam; they turned agonizing eyes toward their masters.

What should they heave overboard? Arguments again arose—shoutings, pullings, and tearings. "No, not the grandfather clock! Not the crate of wine. Not the portraits of Uncle Eli and Aunt Hester. No. No. No."

As they had left the civilized boundaries of home, parts of themselves broke through ordinary armor surrounding ego and soul, broke through surprisingly. Stealth, greed, lust, pushing, shoving, the inner shadows of humanity—unleashed by the unfenced horizons of war.

Esther glanced behind after she and Gerhard abandoned her sewing machine by the roadside, along with a heavy trunk full of quilts, pots, pans, jars, and God-knew-what snatched from the kitchen. She saw a circle of buttocks and bent heads. Arms and hands fought through the trunk for her belongings. She heard the ripping of fine cloth. "This is mine, I got it first." Raucous howlings rose as the ways of civility crumbled.

"Rat-a-tat-tat. Rat-a-tat-tat." The metallic ricochet of a machine gun echoed from somewhere in the woods or beyond the bend. They were beginning to get used to it by now, their sensitivities dulling as they settled in for the inevitable. They knew that many Poles had united with the Russians.

Young Christian, splattered with the mud above his knees, tottered, half-running in an attempt to keep up with Arthur Krahn. Arthur had longer legs but bigger feet, and so was carrying more mud.

Neither boy could say it: "Arthur, Chris, I'm afraid."

A battle-scarred German tank, waving a white flag,

crowded the struggling trekkers. Their wagons pitched and slid precariously on the edge of the drainage ditch.

"Over, over, Elzer. Watch it, Mose."

Esther, thrusting her head and shoulders out from under the canvas, trembled as she saw their plight. "Stop. Stop, Gerhard, or we'll be in the water."

Slowly the horses' feet found solid soil under the seemingly bottomless mud. Sweating they groaned, bringing the wagon back again. It pitched precariously.

As they rounded the bend by the grove of ash and maples, the crowd ahead swarmed to one side. Wails and piercing "Oooohhhh's" rose up.

Ahead were Polish recruits, blood surging at the glory of their newly assigned tasks—assisting the Red Army in corralling the refugees, raiding homes and farms and shooting turncoats and stragglers—especially anyone they decided was a Nazi fascist. Besides, not all of these new Polish "guards" could read the passports and papers flashed before their eyes by trembling hands when they barked, "Papers, papers!"

"Halt. Halt." The words were in Polish. Few of the bewildered refugees could understand.

A group of twelve or so men and women, whose mired or broken-down wagons left them to struggle on foot, were suddenly shoved aside by the cold ends of machine gun barrels. "Over into the woods. Fast. Hurry, you Nazi Fascists."

About half of the group ignored the order. Machine gun fire blazed above their heads. Some fell in the mud. Screams rose, and half of the group fled with mud-caked feet into the woods.

But to their surprise, a Polish woman guard, hatred blazing from her face, yelled out, "There, over there. Betrayers. Fascists."

She fired a volley from her machine gun to let them

know they were now dealing with the unmatched powers of the victors.

Behind, as they turned the bend, the wheel dropped from the rear of Gerhard's wagon. Young Chris, legs weary from plodding in the heavy mud, lurched to Mose and Elzer's side. They trembled, covered with froth, wild-eyed.

"Rat-a-tat-tat." A string of fire zoomed their way from around the bend. A black horse at the wagon ahead crumpled in a heap in his traces.

"We'll have to unhook and turn the team loose." How Gerhard hated saying those words. The last of the farm, the faithful horses. He had turned his blooded stock out of the barn to roam the countryside two days ago. Now this. It had to be done. They could go no farther.

Truth dawned on all the mud-splattered refugees. They could take little with them beyond this point. They were afoot in the cold, battle-scarred, trembling world.

Christian held Grandfather Froese's arm; his right arm dragged a valise Esther had frantically filled with flour, cheese, and a smoked sausage. The rucksack on his back was stuffed with a few clothes.

Esther, mud and water rising above her shoe tops, held Grandmother Froese's left arm with her right as she carried a sack into which she had poked odds and ends in the frenzy. Grandmother Froese's head was dipped in its woolen hood, but her lips still whispered, "Our Father. . . . "

Gerhard gave old Mose a last slap on the side and said his farewell: "Get on, Mose, God take care of you. And Elzer, faithful Elzer—" But as he reached out to touch Elzer, Elzer's dark eyes filmed over. A rush of air spread his nostrils and his feet spread out beneath him. A piece of shrapnel from some wild firings had pierced his heart. Only a tiny trickle of blood marred his satin coat.

There was no time for prolonged farewells. Onward.

Hurry. Lift the ankle above the mud. Totter, plod.

There wasn't even time for Esther to think about what she had feverishly poked into bags and rucksacks. What would they do now? How far to the bridge, to merciful rest in boats?

When they rounded the bend, their legs aching with the struggle, three uniformed Red guards by the edge of the woods called out, "Over here." Again a volley of fire, mercifully over their heads.

"Over here, Fascists." Gun barrels bruised the sides of those in front, gouging, digging.

By now the bone-weary refugees had little resistance. Obey. It couldn't be but a momentary delay. Perhaps someone from the Nazi troops, an officer surely, would be in some shelter to give directions. Oh, for the relief of the determined face of a German officer or guard, his military arm and sure hand directing them.

Chris had given Grandfather's arm to Gerhard. He stepped ahead to rejoin Arthur, whose black hair fell in threads over his sweaty forehead. They lumbered ahead of the family group which brought along the tottering grandparents.

Ahead the earth was ripped open with new trenches. Yes, a battlefield, or a preparation for a battle had been made here by the Germans to guard the approach to the Vistula just ahead.

"Step ahead!" ordered the angry woman, gloating in her soldierly duties.

A small group of three or four refugees marched ahead to the orders. "By the trench, dirty Fascists."

Gerhard and Esther brought up the grandparents, heaving and panting from the excesses of marching in the mud, surrounded by a flock from Schönsee village.

No. It couldn't be. But it was.

"I said, at the trench!" The woman let loose a volley.

Chris hadn't known that human beings, when filled with lead, crumpled to the ground and into the trenches like rag marionettes when the strings are cut. At first he couldn't believe it when they toppled over the edge of the trench.

"Next!" ordered the woman. But her gun needed reloading. She fumbled with her ammunition belt.

Chris never could explain where the strength came from. He only remembered that it seemed like someone whispered in his ear. *Now. Give her a shove. Give her a shove.* It wasn't the voice of the blood-streaked Black Spider. Could it have been Great-grandfather Penner's voice? The grandfather his mother always talked about?

Adrenaline shot through his body. His feet surged out of the sucking mud. Just as she started to turn, her pouting lips ready to bellow another order, Christian Claassen shoved her from the back.

"Run. Run. Father, Mother, all of you, run!"

Behind, the refugees, who had almost lost all hope, now tottered, ran, and dipped for cover in the trees beyond the furious soldier and the sounds of her cursing.

This was their dreadful reality. They were learning that the ways of refugees and war are the ways of chance and accident, the ways of quick decision. Meanwhile, the powers of evil mock and laugh at the piteous creatures scrambling for their lives.

Below the ways of war were its trophies—the glassy eyes, the blackened tongues, and the bloated bellies of the victims, beginning their decay into the earth.

25

"Grab the boat. Hurry!"

The hoards of shoving, lurching, half-frozen refugees leaned over the dark waters of the Vistula. They fell into the small rowboats bobbing drunkenly below.

"In. *Springen!* Jump." The German officer, Willie Lauer, bone-weary with the endless chore of ordering refugees, swung his arms wildly. If a few, probably stinking Poles anyway, fell into the icy waters, what matter. The supply was endless. Where was his relief?

God in heaven! His superior had marched over moments ago to tell him that seven hundred inmates of Stutthof Concentration Camp were released like sewage from a backed-up trough. They'd be pouring into the landing by the afternoon.

Officer Lauer, now bedraggled, moustache dripping, eyes red from too much vodka, swore into the darkness. "Curse the Russians. Curse Herr Hitler. Curse the saboteurs, whoever they were—Jews, Gypsies, Poles. Mennonites? Who are these stinking refugees, anyway?"

Esther, who had lost the extra coat she had been trying to salvage, felt to see if the band around her waist still held the aspirin and the Alpenkräuter (medicinal herbs).

Poor Gerhard. How feeble he looked as the wind blew his pant legs back onto his bony frame. Today, however, the cough had lessened. Why was he sweating so in this cold wind?

"I'll grab the next one." His voice hardly carried to the dozen or so pushing behind Esther, Christian, and the dazed grandparents.

But before Gerhard could grab the next rowboat, someone shoved him aside. Esther saw that they were at the mercy of the desperation war shoves forward. Not the best of human nature. No. The worst of human nature leaked through the cracks in the egos of the famished, exhausted refugees, pushing for survival.

The heads of three who had lost their footing or miscalculated and pitched out of a lurching boat bobbed momentarily in the icy waters. Then, as the bodies swirled, an arm or two appeared, until they were carried away in the silence of the undercurrent.

No time for outcries or bother. Push. Grab a boat.

Only two remained. Esther shoved forward. Her feet were wet and frozen. Her fingers stuck out of her soggy gloves. Grandmother Marie had her hands around Esther's sash, while her feet dragged in the mud. Esther pushed past Gerhard. Somewhere from behind machine-gun fire split the air.

When her green eyes first saw the boats below and the dirty, ghostly figures ahead unchaining them, piling in, setting off amongst the ice floes, a part of her hesitated. "Stealing? We can't steal the boats. These boats belong to someone else. The people of this—" But her words were lost in the shrill wind and the coarse growlings and selfish commands: "Get off. We got here first."

A heavyset man, bulging in his unbuttoned sweater, eyes glaring, raised a paddle. He pounded the fingers of the man who had dared to put a hand on the overfilled boat.

Then Esther recognized that ordinary rules are suspended in times of war and crisis such as this. This boat belonged to someone else; she would have to "borrow" it or be killed by the invading Russians.

Her feet plunged into the frigid water by the dead cattails. "God have mercy. Give me strength." She leaned forward. Her fingers, so cold she could not feel the boards, clasped the very tip of the rocking boat. It was an old one, listing to one side. The very last.

"Mother. Mother." Fear glazed Chris's face as he lurched forward, water up to his waist, placing his hips in front of the unpainted prow. One paddle lay across the rear seat.

By now Gerhard, legs trembling from the chills, had managed to crawl down the bank. He helped Chris and Esther pull the boat close enough for the gasping grandparents to grab hold.

"In first, Gerhard." Esther screamed. Then Chris pushed both grandparents over the edge. Grandmother Marie groaned, losing consciousness. Her tiny body sagged like a half-filled sack of flour in the two inches of water in the bottom of the boat. Grandfather Arnold's precious Bible fell from his hands, and the cold waters swallowed it.

A rush of mud engulfed their feet as the wild-eyed Mennonite refugee from Russia, Cornelius Ewert, slid on his back to the very edge of the black Vistula. He was so shaken by his fall he could only tremble. With his last strength, he gave a heave and fell into the boat alongside grandmother Marie.

Gerhard grabbed the paddle, noticing that it had a broken end. Nevertheless, it was better than nothing. He could actually give a threatening chunk of ice a shove with it. He gripped it tightly, knowing their survival was at stake.

"We stole the boat, Mother. The boat wasn't ours." Chris was bewildered.

"We'll talk about it later. Look for another paddle. Look in the water."

The current caught the tiny craft, swinging it into the rushing waters as they approached the concrete pier that once held the bridge. Some wreckage lingered, bobbing dangerously. If it caught their small craft, they would be overturned. But before they pushed out, seven more people scrambled and clawed their way in.

"Enough! Shove, Chris. Shove, Gerhard! Oh, God above, don't sink us." There were now fifteen people squeezed into the tiny craft designed for not more than five. River water swirled an inch below the boat edge.

Screams rose in the darkness. A crazily bobbing ice floe crashed into the side of the overloaded boat ahead. The boat dipped, obeying the laws of physics. Its crew spilled into the waters so quickly that only the last three had time to scream. Then the cold waters silenced them.

On top of each other, face to face, arms and legs entangled, family and strangers mixed. Silence prevailed, the silence that descends when one is facing death.

"Row. Push!" Chris glanced quickly at his father, who was swinging the broken paddle, trying to guide the boat away from a rock outcropping looming like Gibraltar ahead.

The current carried them within inches of the first rocks. But then again they found their way and joined the current, pushing toward the sea.

Seeing a board, Chris reached out, grabbing for it in the darkness. His fingers slipped. The boat tottered.

"Someone tell the boy to sit still!" snarled the old man with the stocking cap and the black beard.

But at second grasp Chris managed to pull a four-foot piece of floorboard from the debris. Praying for strength, he paddled furiously.

"Father, Father, paddle. Hold. Hold. Paddle."

They were past the rush and dangers of the rocks, joining the irregular shapes bobbing ahead on the angry waters. If God could only send a few stars or an edge of moon to light at least a portion of the frightful darkness.

Ahead, beyond the sandbar at the edge of the rolling water, orange flame from the Russian bombs danced and flashed, but they could take no comfort in such lighting.

26

At one-thirty in the cold blackness of the morning, they had stopped on the sandbar which extended out from the east bank of the Vistula. They huddled in ragged clusters.

Unable to navigate the waters beyond this point because of the threatening ice floes, German guard Willie Lauer circled ahead of the bewildered and frightened refugees with his fellow officer, Wolfgang Fischer—a husky, scar-faced son of Thor, who had mercifully shared his second fifth of vodka with Willie.

The tottering German government had thrust on them this unworthy task of ushering stinking refugees to safety. "God of Thor, God of the Teutons, who on earth likes refugees?" Willie tipped the bottle again, as he waved the trembling survivors to the sandbar.

"*Vorne*. Forward," he rasped, glad to see those who had survived thus far, crash into the sandbar. Soon they both would be relieved of this gaggle of Dutch Werder geese. But then there would be hordes again tomorrow. Whoever would have thought that service in the glorious Reichswehr would end in such nursemaid and suck-bottle-baby-tasks?

Oh, to be in Berlin, as in the old days. Then there were Fräulein in silk stockings, Italian and French wines and champagnes, and the music of Wagner to warm the blood.

Blessedly, when morning dawned there was no gloom of fog. There was no artillery fire or dropping bombs. Ragged and bewildered, they awakened to the day after their fitful attempts to sleep on the cold sand, huddled together to keep from freezing.

"A fire. We must make a fire." Chris, struggling to maintain his balance in his exhaustion, began a search for twigs or driftwood dry enough to burn. Arthur Krahn, who had lost his cap in the mad scramble of the night before, grinned at him, showing bundle of twigs in hands.

"Mother's going to make some tea. She salvaged a pan when we left our wagon, tied it to her sash. She has a little tea and hard rolls in her haversack."

Chris noticed that he didn't say, "Come over for a cup. Warm yourselves." He understood that their problems were too engulfing for ordinary courtesies. He knew the times dictated that Esther Claassen and her brood needed to take care of themselves.

Esther too dug for the stewpan she had been sure to include in her sack, along with a chunk of bacon. They had had to drop the hog shoulders and hams during the last of their trek in the mud.

Her heart sank as she dug for the bacon. There was scarcely enough for two slices left. Famished hordes had descended with outstretched hands yesterday when they had stopped to rest.

"Thank God the sun is shining." She lifted her eyes to the sun above. The sky was cloudless. Spring was on its way. They had been saved from the terrors of the night and of the deep.

They had dropped the bundles with the extra blanket

and coat at the river edge last night. She turned Grandmother Froese so that the sun could shine on her bent back. The old couple, Grandfather now with white whiskers adding ghostliness to his face, leaned on each other. They sighed. "It is *Gottes wille, Gottes wille.*" They were resigned to whatever was, long since knowing they added to Gerhard and Esther's burdens.

"Surely God will take us soon." But strangely, bitterness did not reign in their hearts.

Just as Esther was poking the small stick fire Gerhard had built, pebbles rolled her way, startling her. Turning, she faced a short woman with slouching posture and the same grime on her face that graced them all.

"Well, Esther Claassen. Remember me from back in the Werder?"

It was Jutta Wiehler from the western side of Tiegenhof. The Wiehlers who had once belonged to their own Ladekopp church.

"Why, Jutta Wiehler! You made it?"

Esther's surprise showed in her eyes. She hadn't seen Jutta Wiehler since she and her husband, Horst, had been removed from their church rolls. Horst and Jutta had joined the Nazi party back in the thirties. Their fevered attempts to recruit others in their congregation brought them up against a wall of resistance.

Finally the Wiehlers' frenzies for the Führer had become so demanding, their commitment to the swastika so complete, that church slid to the bottom of their priorities. The church elders dropped the Wiehlers from membership.

"*Grossmutter, Grossvater.*" She dipped her head, covered with a dirty scarf, toward the bent old couple waiting for a sip of hot broth or tea.

Esther resented it, this slouching Nazi woman hovering at the edge of her fire, wanting to visit and be friendly at such a time. Thank God, Jutta hadn't barked "Heil Hitler." Esther's eyes were burning from the smoke of the fire. Right now she needed to make a gruel, some tea for the old folks. She blew on the coals.

"And Christian over there, Frau Esther. My, what a handsome boy he is. Pure Aryan, isn't he? Blue eyes, flaxen hair, broad shoulders. He was in the Youth, wasn't he?"

Esther knew that Jutta and Ernst had a daughter, Hedwig, but she was a year or so older than Chris, wasn't she? Only Hedwig had taken after the Vogt side of the family and had dark hair and complexion, much to Jutta's dismay. Nevertheless, Jutta couldn't resist making an inroad, even at such an inconvenient moment.

"Why, if we tarry long enough here, while our noble supervisors make plans for our safety, they can spend some time together, can't they, Esther? Your Christian and my Hedwig?"

Then Esther remembered. Hedwig Wiehler was almost two years older than Christian. How she crowed to Hermann about her work in the Jungmädel (league of German maidens). And the memory was painful, as such things were not talked about. But Jutta Wiehler talked about it—proudly, as she remembered.

"She's going to give the Führer a son, Esther Claassen. A son for the fatherland. Fathered in the flax field by a healthy, full-blooded Aryan. Hedwig left yesterday for Herr Himmler's Lebensborn Home, the 'Well of Life for the Führer.' "

Jutta's words, spoken without shame, had nearly flattened Esther. But she guessed she was behind the times.

Why wasn't the woman-turned-Nazi over in the cluster of her own family? Where was her pan, her gruel, her coffee or tea?

"Let's visit later, Jutta. I have a feeling there'll be time before we move on again." Esther realized she didn't mean it. Why did she say it? It was the Nazi in Jutta making her bow and cringe.

"Jutta, I need to—" she nodded to the feeble grandparents who had dry throats and trembling hands.

"I don't want to appear rude, but . . . " As Esther turned, the woman in the faded brown dress, with her tokens and rewards for Nazis service still pinned over her bosom, had vanished in the crowd.

Esther reached back for her two strips of bacon. As soon as she poured the grandparents a cup of hot tea in the tin cup she removed from her belt, she'd throw some meal into the boiling water, along with the pieces of bacon mixed with the gruel to warm one's insides.

But when her hand reached the waxed paper where the bacon had rested, her fingers met only the crinkled paper and sand. The bacon had vanished.

She rose. Fury overcame her. Red-hot anger.

"Gerhard, she took the bacon. She stole the bacon. What have we come to? Jutta from the Werder too? I'm going after her."

But Gerhard, feverish, rose to his feet. His long arms and warm hands reached out for his regal wife, now as fiery-eyed as that Norse god Thor himself.

She trembled. Gerhard held her, for she was his stately wife with her crown of auburn hair, her hazel eyes, her culture, her long fingers and the minuets at the piano, her fine desserts at table, her—

Gerhard held her as he felt the sob beginning at the lower part of her bosom heave its way to her throat.

"It's all right, Esther." His hot hands held her shaking back. "All right. So much. We've lost so much. But we're alive. We have each other."

His arms encircled her shoulders. She was comforted by his endearing embrace. When could they have a night as in the old days—their room, sweet with a bouquet of heather; their bed, soft, feathery, rose petals thrown under the pillows? When again?

Enough. The fire popped and crackled. The water boiled. "Chris, come, my son. I'll fix you some hot tea after Grandmother and Grandfather drink theirs."

She tried to bury the thought of that dark-skinned Hedwig Wiehler with her Nazi parents and her League of German Maidens history. God help her if that girl approached Christian, hypnotizing him with those dark eyes, singing, "In the fields and on the heath. . . ."

"Christian. Your tea." Esther didn't realize she barked at him.

27

The beggarly refugees waited there, milling around, crowding, clustering. On the afternoon of the first day on the spit of sand, Russian planes in the clear skies above spotted them and swept low.

This time it was bombs, not strafing. The ground trembled and the waters roiled. Refugees shrieked and ran for any cover. What cover on such an island of sand? There was a stand of willow at the farthest, but not everyone could fit under the low branches.

"The drainage ditch. The drainage ditch!" hollered a half-dozen fleeing youth, Chris among them.

"Mother, Father, the culvert."

Esther swept up her few belongings. Gerhard grabbed a sack. They helped the struggling grandparents to their feet. The grandparents' small steps delayed them, and Esther would not frighten them more by loud screaming and frantic hurrying. "God preserve us," she prayed.

They were among the last to crawl under the edge of the culvert. The boom and thunder of the explosions, the blast and swish of the sand, deafened them.

"Oh, my God. Oh, my God!" The despairing cries rose as those who found safety focused their unbelieving eyes on bodies, those caught still running, rising into the air, then falling shattered into the sand craters.

"Christian. Where's Christian?" Esther's eyes pierced the gloom of the tunnel, trying to identify the rumpled, disheveled heads.

"I'm here, Mother, back here with Hedwig. We made it safely." His voice echoed in the dank tunnel.

Christian sat beside the dark maiden with her golden Bund Deutscher Mädel honor award still pinned on her shoulder.

How comforting it felt, her throbbing, warm hand in his. Soft, feminine. Not hardened and calloused with grimy knuckles like the hands of so many German women in these distressing times.

Hedwig tightened her grip on the young man's hand. She wondered whom had it caressed? Warm blood pulsed through their veins; their energetic hearts beat faster. The blood throbbed in the strong vein at the side of Christian's throat, a throat her lips sought to kiss.

As Hedwig moved closer to him, he caught some trace of woman smells—a hint of perfume? After the muddy march, the sweat? What was happening to him? It was as if his body was trying to twist out of his control. He knew he couldn't talk just then; his voice would quiver too much.

"Hedwig, Hedwig—" But that was all his tongue could say just then. He wanted to say, "Hedwig, let's run, run in the sunshine, roll in the golden sand, climb the swaying willows, laugh and pull at purple grapes together with our teeth until our lips touch." His blue eyes opened to see the brown pools of her eyes holding his.

There was an earsplitting boom, then the swish of sand. Clods fell at the entrance of the tunnel only a few feet away as another bomb fell.

"We're safe, Christian. We're safe. And Chris, it isn't over. This is cowardly fleeing. In time Herr Hitler will send reserve officers, real Reich officers and generals. You'll see these mongol Russians dissolve in the sand before your eyes. Heil Hitler! We have been taught to sing the songs of triumph. We ourselves, the Hitler Youth, are triumphant. Heil Hitler!" Hedwig snuggled in, head under Chris Claassen's chin.

Surprisingly, here and there down the avenue of the culvert, mostly from fuzzy-cheeked youth, rose the click of tongue in response: "Heil Hitler." Their long years of training programmed their tongues for automatic response.

No, it was not over. In Berlin, in Frankfurt, in Hamburg, in cities with buildings split and stones and bricks filling the streets, carefully groomed Nazi officers furtively packed their bags as they colluded and schemed among themselves. "Underground, underground. To Paraguay, to Brazil, even to America. Wherever. The swastika will triumph. This is only temporary. What glorious powers of nation and Reich we have spawned, sown with such ecstasy and burst of soul, such Nürnberg might and holy hush! *Sieg heil!* (hail to victory). We will triumph."

The afternoon was spent burying the dead from the bombings in the sand, while the cold wind blew from the north over the dark waters.

Pastor Malcolm Hege of the Mennonites of the Vistula Delta, land of the old Dutch settlers, stood at the common trench. Fourteen bodies were spread out below. One was the skin-and-bones body of poor old Cornelius Ewert, refugee from Russian terrors, resting in peace at last. It was not strange that there was little weeping. They had suffered at the reckless hands of war too long. Their sensitivities were dull, slipping underground. The closing in of psyche and spirit was needed for their survival.

The German cutter boats had not yet arrived on the third day. They would plow through the heavy ice floes, taking the refugees to the waiting whaling vessels just off the coastal ice. "When? When? " Their hearts were restless with the waiting.

The bombings had ceased, and in their place the rats of hunger gnawed at their guts. Esther had scraped the last of the flour into the water for a thin paste. She had thrown in a half-handful of beans, emptying the last from the sack. But that was last evening. Today they had only water, boiled and served in her tin cup.

Though weakening, somehow the grandparents seemed to preserve their strength. They leaned against each other, eyes pondering the sand.

"We need time to talk about it, talk about it." Grandfather Arnold's voice rose above its usual old man's rasp. He sounded almost youthful, and his eyes glistened.

"Too much. Too quick. We rode along on the crest. When?" He looked at Gerhard, then over to Esther. "When will we talk about it?"

Yes, when? Gerhard, cheeks flushing from fever, agreed. When? They had been swept along. Not just the Lutherans and the Catholics, but they too had been swept along, they who had brought to the Werder a believer's faith focused on a Savior going to a cross. This other cross, this swastika—what had it wrought?

Gerhard was unaware, until Esther touched his soiled pants leg, that he was talking out loud. "Romans 13. Romans 13. We misunderstood Romans 13. Did we adjust the Scripture so that we could march in tune with all the rest?"

Feeling Esther's hand, he turned. He looked into her pained hazel eyes. He gazed at her auburn hair, now streaked, strands falling; at her torn and dirty skirt; at the sweater around her shoulders, snagged and burr-laden. Esther, his pretty one, his regal one. His Esther before

King Ahasuerus. Why had not one among them said, "Who knoweth whether thou art come to the kingdom for such a time as this?"

Grandfather Froese was right. Through his feeble flesh the spirit still called. When, when would their tongues be loosened? When would they look each other in the eyes and talk about it, talk about the reign of the Black Spider? They had climbed on the broad board of Romans 13, mouthing "obey those who rule over you . . . government is instituted of God." They were swept into the embrace of the Black Spider. Would any of them survive?

On the second cold evening, while the refugees still waited, their German guides fortified and warmed themselves with more vodka, Chris and Hedwig sat by the Wiehler fire. Chris knew that soon he should return to his own fire. His parents would be worried. Yet he lingered.

Maybe Hedwig was right. This was only temporary. A flaw in the glorious system of the Third Reich which would soon be whisked away. A storm, though a fierce one, before the final dazzling dawning.

Chris again felt the surge of strength, the power of the Reich, the standards, the flags. But hadn't he flinched a little at the Black Spider? Hadn't a part of him sensed its poison?

This turning the other cheek like that faith confession he read that day—it sounded so laughable, weak, futile. How can the governments of the world rule by turning the other cheek? And what are governments? Where do they begin? And their blood, Aryan blood—hadn't scientists from their own people of the Werder proven its superiority?

What about his brother, Hermann, stalwart, clear-eyed, strong. "Oh God, where is Hermann?" But it was only a thought, not a prayer. Who really believed in a God above? Hedwig was right. The old god of Thor, the god of power, fist, and might, the god that did not flinch at blood but grabbed the standard and marched on, trampling on the ranks of the half-human subspecies—Jews, Gypsies, Bohemians. Didn't it make sense to cleanse a society of the feebleminded and freaks of nature? Who could look at them anyway?

"Christian." Hedwig's firm hand reached for his arm. "Come by the fire. Luckily we have meat for supper."

Her smile, her dark eyes, and dark skin, reminded him of that Jewish girl who had lived with them a while back. The trek, the pain, the whirling events had made him almost forget that Jewish girl. What was her name? Too bad Hedwig didn't look more Aryan. But some of Herr Hitler's inner circle of Aryans were dark-haired, weren't they?

He wasn't mature enough to put it into words or fully recognize this first love of adolescence brought about by circumstance, accident, and crowding, braced by a young body throbbing with life.

He was about to say, "Hedwig, I must go to my family. Maybe they need me," but he smelled the roasting flesh. Meat. My God, meat! And his stomach had shrunk into a knot. Only water all day. Chris couldn't resist. He rose to let Hedwig lead him to the crackling fire.

"Meat for a real Aryan Jungvolk" (Hitler youth guard) said Jutta Wiehler proudly. She ripped off the front leg of the muskrat which had been roasted on a small branch over the fire.

His saliva flowed as his hand lurched forward, almost beyond conscious control.

28

They scrambled aboard the whaling vessel *Witzell*, a rusty, forty-year-old ship corralled by the German Refugee Service along with a fleet of similar ships anchored in the ice floes. Beyond, in the fog and dismal rain which had just begun, bobbed the equally rusty *Esser* and the *Riefenstahl*.

Admiral Doenitz of the German Admiralty ordered every available navel vessel, as well as privately owned boats, to the ports of Pillau and Hela in the Gulf of Danzig—in all, 790 ships.

It was Dunkirk again. This time, however, it was not English soldiers who were fleeing like rats toward the crazed assortment of dinghies, cutters, fishing vessels, and whatever else floated at the northern coast of France. No, the waiting whalers were filling with refugees, despairing mothers, children, grandparents, and fathers, many bearing scars or stumps where there had been arms or legs. They shoved, scuttled, bent and bowed, these hordes. They did not yet understand what the word *refugee* meant nor what the future held for them.

There were praying people, people of the Werder farms. There were fat merchants, seeking to save both body and bank account. There were half-hidden Nazis, whose swastika arm bands lay only slightly beneath the surface of their paltry baggage.

As they boarded the *Witzell*, Captain Schilzer and his dismayed crew frantically waved futile directions to the hordes flowing in. Decks designed for sixty would soon groan with two thousand.

"God in heaven, God in heaven, we will sink!" The captain moaned, yet they poured like gray rats across the last gangplank. Some went to blessed refuge in west Germany. Some died in the cold darkness below the ice floes, as Allied submarines, like slow-roving sharks, swept along the bottom of the bay.

Gerhard and Esther tried to hover around the fragile grandparents, who bore the tide of events almost courageously. Pitiful old Beulah, half out of her mind, stumped along on her infected corns, muttering, "Holy Mother of Jesus." She had lost her beads in the scramble back at the sandpits.

Christian held the haversacks and their pitiful belongings. He looked back worriedly. "Hedwig, Hedwig." He searched, he called. There was no reply. He could not see, as the dank fog engulfed them. They all looked the same, these vagabond travelers—mournfully and hopelessly lost.

"She'll make it on one of the other vessels, son, if they pull the gangplank for this one. Maybe she went on ahead."

Esther didn't say it in the push and rush to find a corner for her small brood, but she hoped Hedwig Wiehler and her Nazi parents did not shove their way on this ship.

"No, don't go after him," Gerhard had said last evening, when she waited for Christian by her fire to drink herb tea from her pot. That Chris should go to Hedwig's fire without telling them still galled her.

163

But Gerhard was right. "Don't fan the flames by searching. Don't criticize Hedwig or her family. Try to bear it."

Esther knew Gerhard was right. Forbidding the young Chris to see Hedwig would be like opening the door of the pigeon cote on a spring morning. He would only fly faster to her. She understood. Chris must find out on his own.

When he finally came to their fire last night, she could see it in his eyes—the difference, the change. Something of his innocence was gone. It had to happen. She had been surprised that it hadn't occurred earlier, in the Jugend. The pressures on the adolescents, the full-blooded young men and the sultry, energetic maidens, were strong.

How he had changed. To Esther, it was like stepping back to the ancient times of the wild-blooded rushings of the ancient gods—Thor, Balder, and Wotan. She tried not to hate Nazi Hedwig and her loose ways.

"Here, Mother, Father. Bring Grandmother and Grandfather over here."

Grandmother staggered and would have pitched to the deck, but Gerhard caught her. They found a little corner by a towering, rusty iron basin used to boil down the whale blubber. They sagged to the deck. Fortunately the rim protected them from the cold rain falling from the Baltic sky.

Still no sight of Hedwig. The captain had pulled the gangplank, angry that twenty or thirty more than he had accounted for had slipped aboard.

Steam rushed. Smoke billowed from the stack. Chill wind blew over the wall-to-wall grayness—the gray faces and gray clothes of the refugees, the gray sky, the gray ship. God in heaven. What was keeping the ship and the war-weary refugees from slipping into gray nothingness?

Underneath, however, there were heartbeats of hope. There were still prayers to the heavenly Father and prayers to Christ. There were Catholic fingers on beads and a grandmother was saying the "Our Father." Now that their feet were on a small but substantial deck, the hope rose, like the flame of a candle almost but not quite blown out by the agonies of the sandbar, the strafings, the bombings, the rat-gnawing hunger.

Blarings reverberated. The raspy-throated, bewildered Captain Schilzer took command, knees knocking in the cold. "Breakfast at seven in the morning. At twelve o'clock, a bowl of soup. Six in the evening, bread and water. Bowel and bladder movements for men and women at opposite ends of the decks. Yonder," he swung his wet arm toward the aft of the vessel, "the canvas sheet covers the barrels for the women. To the fore," he swung his arm forward, "behind the canvas are places for men."

"We'll be having dung and vomit dripping from one end of the decks to the other," he growled to his mate. Oh, for the open sea, the tropical isles, the old times, the white-capped waves, the blowing whales, the slick-skinned beauties on the islands.

Chris knew by now that he had lost Hedwig. "She'll be on the other ship, won't she, Father?"

"Yes, son. The Wiehlers know how to take care of themselves. They are survivors." Gerhard reached out, placing his arm around the broad shoulders of his son.

Gerhard himself knew the pain, the struggle his young son was enduring through these distortions of time, of values, of beliefs brought on by the god of war. He himself had been down the dark, thorn-enclosing path. "The *Esser* and the *Riefenstahl* are just ahead of our ship. I believe they must have boarded ahead of us. You'll meet again."

He knew it was reassurance, and reassurance amounted to little more than a soggy piece of driftwood. Nevertheless, Chris needed all the hope he could muster.

What was there to do now? Two or three days on this vessel to west Germany, maybe more, depending on the weather. *Give yourself to the moment,* Esther thought to herself. Someday, like Grandfather Arnold said, they must discuss it. Discuss it seriously.

The cries of children rose with the shrieks of the descending gulls. Now underway, the ship rocked in the waves of the high sea. Coal smoke billowed, then blew back, settling on them. They coughed, hacked, spit, and vomited. Those unfortunates who did not make it to the canvassed corners or icy rails soiled and wet their clothes.

There was no order at all. No one knew whether all the grimy extended hands received their evening slice of bread. Who but God above could know, with such shoving, such crazy crowding?

"What does the government think I'm supposed to do?" wailed the captain helplessly. He hurried to his cabin to unlock the liquor cabinet.

Rain descended throughout the night. Esther and Gerhard pushed the aged ones beneath the edge of the iron basin above them. Mercifully they were able to keep them dry.

Chris held his knees with blue-cold hands. He had lost his gloves somewhere back on the sandpits, cavorting with Hedwig. Lost his innocence too.

Fitfully he slept, maybe for half an hour. And the Black Spider came to him, legs roiling like serpents or a giant octopus. The center body swelled bloodred, the red of the flag of the Reich on which the Black Spider writhed. The eyes bulged, and a leering smile spread below.

Chris caught his breath, then his chest heaved, panting as the dream entangled him. Instead of the bulging head of the spider or the octopus, Hedwig Wiehler's face rose up. The tentacles elongated and writhed, seeking to pull him close to Hedwig's red mouth and laughing eyes.

Then she spoke. "Nazi. Beautiful word, Chris. Beautiful word. Stay with me, and we shall change your name.

The old one, Christian, is unsuitable. Have you not been taught that the ancient, crawling, demeaning, weak, and supplicating way has passed? Come. Come, come to the true cross, my swastika. Drink of the blood of the true Aryan God. I shall change your name to Thor."

Hedwig's face disappeared. Her full, blood-red lips, which had pressed his in feverish kisses, vanished. The swastika swirled, smothering him.

He woke with a gasp. Glad he had not cried out and wakened the others, he adjusted his numb buttocks and legs. He buried his chin on his hands to ponder his dream. A wetness in his pants told him his body had responded to the intoxicating dream.

As he bowed his head, golden hair wet, he could smell the sweat and salt on his body. Opening his chapped lips slowly, he mouthed a prayer: "Our Father who art in heaven. . . ."

The bean soup and moldy bread turned Esther's stomach. The soup had been only cloudy hot water, with one bean, hard as a pebble, on the bottom of her tin cup.

Nevertheless, she was bloated. Her guts roiled. Pains shot up and down her belly. She knew she'd have to try to struggle through the hordes on the deck to the aft portion and that stretched sheet of canvas. No. She wasn't prepared yet to let go where she was, as some of the poor compromised unfortunates had to do.

It took her almost ten minutes of agony to get there, with the ship pitching as it was and the rails lined with gagging, vomiting victims.

To the left, maybe to the right also, were those whose innards roiled with power and frenzy couldn't wait for the line and the privacy of the canvas. She lowered her eyes at dislodged clothing and bare buttocks sticking out over the frigid rails. Stench and groans rose in the wind.

Finally, the canvas sheet. Only eight or nine ahead of her. God be merciful. She tightened her thighs to control the body she inhabited. Had it come to this? Would she have to shove herself to the rail before her turn?

A woman from the Danzig flats, breath strong enough to drop a gull, leered at her. "Makes a lady step high, don't it, ma'am?" Then she snickered.

Poor soul. But me too, thought Esther. *Me too. I stink. I'm in rags. Belongings? I have none. Oh, my beautiful home on the Werder. My spacious, rose-filled home. My home of sons and loving husband.*

Then, mercifully, the canvas was pushed back as an old babushka waddled past, black gap showing through the grin on her wrinkled face. "Your turn, your highness," she cackled, as if addressing the queen.

Esther's chapped hand grabbed the edge of the wind-blown cloth, drawing it back. Mercifully, there were two barrels. But one was occupied. "Why, bless my soul," said the occupant, "if it isn't Queen Esther Claassen from Schönsee on the Werder."

"Olga. Olga Fritzenheimer. How on earth? My God, what are you doing here?"

29

"Seat yourself before you're shoved over the railings, Queen Esther. We're all brought low. No white enameled bowl, water, and pull-chain. What does the Bible say? The high places shall be made low?"

The dirty sheet was pulled back. "Who do you think you are, the queen climbing on her throne? Get on with it," rasped an angry woman in the line behind.

Humiliated beyond belief, Esther got up on the barrel near Olga.

"Oooooh. Ooooooh." Olga Fritzenheimer held her head, covered with the dirty straw of her hair. "Oooooh, ooohh. The fever. The fever. The pain. My innards. OOOOOOOhhhhhhh."

Esther relieved herself. Then, brushing down her clothing, she turned to the rolling, apparently sick human being imploring her with those pale blue eyes.

"Olga, what can I do?" She offered to help. She had the blood of the good Samaritan flowing in her veins.

But then she thought, *Her baby. Where is her baby? Olga would have a small child by now, surely.*

"Olga, you were with child. Where is your baby?"

"Oh, the child? Yes. I lodged in Herr Himmler's

Lebensborn Home, a veritable well of life for the Führer. But, Frau Claassen, the infant died soon after birth. Grief-stricken. You're beholding a grief-stricken mother."

Again the canvas was turned back. "My turn. Get on with it. We all have diarrhea, not locked bowels. Get on with it."

Esther reached toward Olga, who had lumbered off her perch. She was bent over, her grief apparently overcoming her.

"A bonnie baby boy, Frau Claassen. A fine, fair-skinned man-child for the Führer."

Her sobbing overwhelmed her. Esther extended the rag she held in her hand. Enemy or not, this was a time for intervention. She embraced Olga with her stinking dress and lice-infested hair. Embraced her. Olga had long ago removed her Nazi uniform, knowing the Red avengers might pierce her through if they caught her.

"Olga. Olga, poor Olga." Esther knew the endless pain of losing a child.

"The little lad lived a month, Esther. I named him Siegfried. The great Wagner opera you know, the one the Führer loved so well. Siegfried. One month with his mother. Those invading Russian soldiers brought infectious diseases. Yes, that's why he died. Nasty Russian diseases. Ohhhhh, I can see its sweet, innocent face yet, smiling at its mother. Oh, little Siegfried."

"Olga, Olga, how can I help?" Esther felt helpless. What could she offer?

"Frau Claassen, do you have any medicine? Any aspirin? Anything for this gut-bloating fever?" Her breath reeked in Esther's face. Obviously she was sick.

"I do." A part of her pulled at the other part of her. *Don't do it, Esther. Your family may need the aspirin and bottle of Alpenkräuter tucked in your waistband.*

"Here. Open your hand, Olga."

Two women pushed into the enclosure, lurching forward to perch on the barrels.

"Oh, mercy, mercy of Thor and Wotan. Medicine." Her hands grabbed the gifts of mercy. Her pale eyes looked sick, and a ring of grime ran slick around her neck. "Oh my. Heeeeeee," Olga hooted, shoving Esther back on the uncovered deck into the crowds.

"You pitiful, scraping, bow-the-neck-and-knee weak Jesus lover. You miserable example for the Third Reich. Your own family should nail you to the barn door, Esther Claassen, giving your medicines away."

Pulverized with shock and fear, Esther tried to step back, away from the body shoved against her bosom, the face sneering at her. Tricked again.

"Olga, the baby—"

"You fool. Fool! It was a poor, wrinkled little devilish thing. Dark-skinned and hairy. Bless Thor. It lived only a day. How I despised it. *Bless Thor.* I'm glad it's dead. *Glad.*"

She shoved her lips closer to Esther's face.

"Poisoned. Poisoned, Esther Claassen. Poisoned by my staying with yellow-bellied Werder folks like you Mennonites. And, that *Jew girl* put a curse on it while it was in my womb. A curse."

The ship twisted and rolled. Esther fell to the deck along with a dozen others. While she was struggling to her feet, the momentary gap in the crowd closed. Her eyes searched. Olga Fritzenheimer had disappeared.

Throughout that cold afternoon, they rode the waves in silence, many so seasick they feared for their very lives. Grandfather Arnold's heart began missing beats, then speeding up in strange palpitations.

"Over, move over."

Gerhard said it as kindly as he could. Anyone could see the old man was failing fast and needed space where they could stretch his body.

They tried to cooperate, these unfortunate ones who were fleeing the red flag of the hammer and sickle and its terrors. They pressed back. Give the dying a space. It wouldn't be long, anyway. Maybe their turn. Who knew?

Grandmother Froese, seeing her stricken old husband, lifted her eyes, "Yeah though I walk through the valley of the shadow—"

She was resigned to the hour. Both she and Arnold, stripped of earthly things, homeland and hearth, were now stripped of time. She held the gnarled hand, already losing color.

Then Grandfather Froese's heart stopped beating. There is a time and place for everything; this heart knew its time. The sweetness of a smile graced the white-bearded face, as if he had stepped across a river like the Vistula into the Werder or a land even greener.

30

Esther was proud of Gerhard. Thin, beggarly looking though he was, yet there was always that character about him. His words were few, his thoughts were deep, and his resolutions, once made, were unwavering. Through strands falling over her hazel eyes, she watched him weaving through the throngs to the captain's office.

"Father. Papa, my papa." The words, spoken only in whispers, drifted over the old man's body, past the black-clothed grandmother, who was relieved though grieving.

She saw her childhood home on the Werder, the other side of Schönsee. Peaceful village. Beautiful village. It was as if the hymns of the gathered worshipers in the little Werder congregation wafted over her.

Though there was dull grayness above, grayness surrounding her, grayness beneath, still there was this shaft of light illuminating her heart.

Smoke swirled from the stack above her head. The blast of the foghorn mocked their bewildering fate. Yet there was this light, these angelic sounds of her people singing.

"I hear the singing on the Werder in the little church,

Mother. Do you hear it too? "

"Yes, my daughter, Esther. I hear it too. It has sustained me all the way." Her cracked, salty lips opened and, surprisingly, her voice sounded young and clear. Esther joined her and they sang,

> Jesus, still lead on, till our rest be won,
> And, although the way be cheerless,
> We will follow, calm and fearless;
> Guide us by thy hand to our fatherland.

Two bowing shipmates returned with Gerhard, edging through the crowd, staggering when the ship heaved.

"Our condolences, ma'am. *Grossmutter.*" They nodded, sincere, but their emotions were now dull as weathered wood from this trek morning and afternoon and God-knows-when to pick up the ones who did not survive the night.

"Open up, make way." They walked slowly through the throng with Grandfather Froese's body on their stretcher. They slipped the body into a paper sack, dropping it into the swinging lifeboat along with a dozen more. Tomorrow some father, some reverend would say the words and read the service. It mattered little to them.

When they ate their evening slice of sawdust bread, heads bending with the dipping of the ship, Gerhard said, "We have to stay together. Nothing in the world is as important as family. Church, yes. But isn't church family also? Our church, our family—Christian for generations."

He didn't say it, but he was thinking it: *The body of Christ. The church, the families in the church, the Christ drawing them. Truly, the body of Christ.*

"As we confess," he said aloud, "we have sinned and come short of the glory of God. Still, still he leads us."

His blue eyes searched young Christian's face. "It is

idolatry, my son, when his people worship and bow down to the god of the nation. Some of our elders rose up. They proclaimed this truth. Now we see how right they were. Still I know Christ has not abandoned us."

Never had Esther heard Gerhard speak words so filled with the holy. He had always kept these things within. She reached out for his hand, noticing it was feverish again.

Thankfully they all slept more that night. The rain had stopped. By now they were used to the ship's movements. Here and there the cry of a child rose up. An edge of moon split a graceful shaft upon the deck, enough to give hope.

In her dream, Esther was ten, auburn hair flying behind her as she raced with a graceful father toward the meadow. Buttercups danced before her. He took her hand, this father who had stood by the piano as she practiced her scales, the hymns, the minuets, and chorales of Bach.

The cold world awaited all of them when they awakened.

The cup of hot water. What was it called? Tea? Coffee? Neither. But it and the piece of bread filled a corner of the shrunken stomach and warmed the bones, preparing them for the blessed event—the cup of soup at noon.

Above the gray of morning sky and fog, the bombers droned. Russian? British? American? God knew.

And the *Esser*, the *Witzell*, and the *Riefenstahl* plowed on, steaming along with similar cargoes of lice-infested passengers.

"Boom. Roar. Boom, boom!" Ocean waters rose above the fog. Horns blared in distress like dying whales. They could only hear the gurgling wails of the *Riefenstahl*, as it took its pitiful cargo to the bottom of the Baltic Sea.

Young Christian, startled by the bombs, leaped to his feet, eyes straining to see in the gloom. "Hedwig, Hedwig. Oh, Jesus, Hedwig!"

31

Two hundred of them crowded into the small school auditorium in the village of Eckenferter.

"Safe. Safe. Gerhard, thank Jesus above. I feel like saying, 'Who hath believed our report? To whom hath the arm of the Lord been revealed?' "

Though he did not say it, Gerhard's heart responded to Esther's words. Even beyond her words. With grimy hand he reached over and drew Esther closer to his side. His eyes, open with hope, looked into hers.

"Esther, we can begin again. We will. I've always wanted to open a clock and watch store. You know how I tinkered with the broken clocks and watches of the folks back home."

"Yes, Gerhard. Yes." Anything. What matter. God had brought them through the ordeal. Even though her father's body had been lowered into the sea, she could put it in its place. In his own time, Grandfather had died. Died with a smile on his lips. His death taught her that even a refugee can die in peace.

"Do you think it was because he saw the Lord, the Lord of the peace he always talked about? A way of sacrifice and of the cross?"

She thought about it as the orange sun pushed over the eastern horizon. Soon there would be the confusion of all the refugees lumbering, crying, hustling for a crumb, or a cup of hot water. How? When? Mercy, mercy. When could they take a bath, or even wash their hair? She hated to do it, but her hand went to her scalp for unbecoming scratching. Lice.

The refugee director had said they would be given instructions on delousing. She had leaned on Gerhard, face in his shoulder as she snickered about it. Her? Delousing? Her family bedbug-ridden? Lice-laden?

"Mother, tell them to hurry. What a relief it'll be." Christian raked under his arms.

Christian was crestfallen and in his own way grief-stricken. Yet how could he know? It could be that Hedwig and her parents were behind them, or that she was on the *Esser* instead of the *Riefenstahl*.

Esther's heart ached for her boy. His eyes were cast down. His feet dragged his tired body and tattered clothes.

She hoped that with the bustle and the newness of their escape from the worst of the dangers, he would be caught by the new—new friends, new lodging, new work, and in time a new school. New meeting with Hermann! Oh, merciful God, was Hermann safe too?

Old Beulah and Grandmother Froese sat by the dingy wall. Beulah's snaggle-toothed mouth worked up and down, fostering the flow of saliva to moisten her leathery lips and tongue.

"We're true sisters now. The blessed crucified heart of Jesus brought us together, her and me." Old Beulah held the hand of her newly adopted charge, Grandmother Froese, who seemed willing to allow herself the ministrations of the old Polish Catholic woman.

"I know faith when I see it. You are a woman of faith. Yes. Catholic or Mennonite or Lutheran, we all are leveled by war. The Christ we turn our eyes on is the same for us all. Isn't that right, Beulah?"

Why, if Beulah insisted, Grandmother would hobble along right beside her to a Catholic chapel in this village. She'd seat herself and pray, while the old woman in the black scarf knelt for her communion.

Would the days of communion when the Werder Mennonites took the cup and the bread come again? She realized she needed it. Yes. She must tell Gerhard that when they got settled they must find a church for Christian and themselves. Oh, God. Could they ever have a church of their own faith again?

But it seemed everybody despised refugees.

"What'll we feed them?" asked the villagers of Eckenferter, some resentfully.

But even with their own destitute conditions, volunteers from the village found grace enough in their hearts to open a small serving area. They offered hot water with a rank smell, called coffee, and that all-too-common bread made of God-knows-what.

The rest of the day they regrouped into their families, their survival groups. They counted their worldly possessions. By now, distanced from angry sea waters and the bombs at least temporarily, they could laugh.

"Pasteboard? Anyone know where I can get pasteboard for my shoes?"

"Why, would you look what I still have in my haversack, a second pair of drawers." Then hysterical laughter, while they scraped backsides where lice asserted themselves.

Then there were some who set their chins. "Delousing! God above. No, I will not subject myself to anything so dishonorable." But time unraveled such thoughts, especially when the lice, hatched from the eggs laid nights before in body hair, dug in for blood.

"When you get back from delousing," called the manager of the refugees, "you will all be transported to the town of Damendorf. This village is too small for so many refugees. Your opportunities will be better in Damendorf." What he meant was that two of the village councilmen threatened to string him up if he didn't shove the dirty vagabonds on somewhere else.

Chris brightened when he bumped into Arthur Krahn struggling in a school restroom to bring order to his disheveled, dirty hair. He had splashed cold water on his face, removing the first layer of the grime.

"Chris!" called Arthur. "You made it. I came on the *Esser*. Somehow after the bombing we got behind your ship. You all right?"

Chris grabbed Arthur's's hand. "Arthur, Arthur, we can go together."

And they did. With nothing substantial in their bellies, new hope livened in their steps.

"We prefer to walk, Mother," Chris called to Esther and Gerhard, as they rode by in the old backfiring truck. "We'll meet you at the delousing center." They bent over in hysterics. Boys again.

Arthur dug under his armpits. "Chris, did you ever itch like this before? Aren't you ashamed, having lice?"

If time had permitted, they would have taken time to roll in the grass alongside the road. Roll and laugh. Laugh outrageously, adolescently. Laugh at the inroads and outroads of life.

"Next," commanded the refugee officer. "Next. Not more than fifty. Watch it."

Citizens of Damendorf resented too that they had to aid such stinking, hopeless ones. God knew there wasn't enough food for their own tables. And who wanted to eat while a wild-eyed, starving refugee, a stinking one at that, looked in your kitchen window at you?

But at least some of the citizens were concerned enough to help set up the delousing center. They themselves had suffered. Dead sons. Dead fathers and daughters. Mothers famished and languishing. Glorious flag toppling. Tables nearly bare. Horse meat, if you could find it.

They lined up Esther Claassen, the hobbling elderly ones at her side, and the forty-or-so other women, looks of despair and shame on their faces. "God, have mercy. Never in our born days did we foresee standing in line for lice removal."

The group ahead of them was especially foul-looking. Such godforsaken people. Were those stripes?

"Beulah, are those some kind of uniforms those poor creatures just ahead are wearing?"

Beulah belched loudly from the cup of sick coffee she had swilled too fast. The moldy bread rolled in her bloated belly.

"Why, Mrs. Claassen, I do believe it is. Believe them there's them uniforms what they put on the camp prisoners. You know, concentration camps. Better stay back from them people. God only knows—thieves, prostitutes, crazy people. You know. Jews. How'd they get loose, anyway?"

A truck, packed with more waifs and lost ones, pulled in behind their line. It backfired, startling them. Among those who turned back, focusing widened eyes on the fracas, was a thin, weaving, wispy little creature. Her eyes seemed larger, darker than the others. What made her look so grotesque, among the stinking ones around her, was the way her bones poked through the striped rags she wore. She did not fall, though she looked as if a breath of the April air would have sent her toppling.

Her eyes caught the eyes of the tall woman back there with the two old ones tottering beside her. She was reminded of someone she had once known.

"Get on. They've opened the door for our group," the

ghoul behind her rasped.

The eyes, still feverish, glistening through the rims of grime, focused again. "My God. God of Abraham! Shema, Israel, there is a God who answers prayer. Mother Esther, Mother Esther." The waif fell to the planks beneath.

But Ruth was not unconscious. She didn't know how Esther managed to slide through the crowd and the line, but there she was—Esther Claassen bending over the Jewish girl, Ruth Rosenbaum.

"Oh, Ruth. Ruth. I thought you were lost forever. Yes, Ruth. Shema, Israel, Oh, nothing in heaven or earth shall separate us again."

32

After the lurching ride back from the delousing center, Esther had to leave Ruth Rosenbaum in her weakened condition. She was leaning against the wall across from the sunny window in the shabby tavern dance hall, space apportioned by who got there first.

"It is like sitting by Galilee or Jordan. Yes, Mother Beulah and Grossmutter Marie and I shall pray while you find food. God of mercy." Her voice faded, and her head dropped on her breastbone as she slept. There would be time for her accounts of suffering later.

To begin again with nothing means to start with the most important thing first: food. Lodging, though temporary, was provided. It was a bed of straw on a small dance-hall floor but a refuge, nevertheless.

"They're giving away shoes, Mother, in front of the hardware store across the way. Art and I are hurrying over. See?"

Chris held up his foot. The ties had long dissolved in what was left of the eyelets of his high-topped shoes. The toe of one shoe flapped as he walked. Esther could see the skin of his foot through the big hole in the bottom of the left one.

"Go, my son. Shoes. Yes."

She'd have to find something to substitute for stockings. She kept a watchful eye for stray cloth, old rags, drifting or scattered here and there.

Both Chris and Art hooted in surprise, "Wooden shoes. Wooden shoes. How can a person walk in wooden shoes?"

But the insides were softly carved and fit the shape of the foot.

"Not bad at all." Clomp, clomp, clomp. Their feet, unaccustomed to the unyielding wood, dragged across the cobblestones.

"Oh, dancing shoes. Dancing shoes." Chris kicked his thin long leg into the air. But he had miscalculated; the shoe went sailing across the middle of the cobblestone street.

"Stockings. Art, we need stockings."

They howled, they rolled in the middle of the street, until the clompings of a team of horses drawing another wagonfull of refugees sent them rolling toward the side by the dance hall where they temporarily lodged.

Esther laughed too. She bent over, holding her sides. She had forgotten the release of laughter, the blessed rippling through the whole body. It was cleansing, healing.

"Loan them to me, son, and I shall do a minuet." Esther howled with the boys. Their stomachs were gnawing again. Tattered clothing blew against their bones as Esther Claassen, Mennonite woman of the Werder, stepped out of her run-down brogues and planted her calloused feet in the wooden enclosures. She lifted the unraveled hem of her skirt and kicked up her heels.

Exhausted in a minute, they collapsed on the curb.

"Oh my, We have to go, boys. We have to go. Search for food. Yes. We have to begin somewhere."

Esther and Gerhard went to the little farm with the row

of basswood trees along the lane. Farmer Wert had offered the committee his fields for gleaning.

Art and Christian took the field across the dirt road leading out of Eckenferter, the field of long-past harvested beets. Sack in hand, hope in their hearts, they sallied forth to rummage.

They could not endure it more than an hour. Fatigue drew them to the cold ground. Even the spring wind bore heavily on their frames.

Mercy prevailed. When Esther joined the others who shared the top of the iron stove in their corner, her pot was filled with water and slices from the mostly rotten beets the boys had salvaged.

The gruel was thickened with the handful of wheat she and Gerhard had managed to glean in Farmer Wert's field. A smile spread across Esther's face. Now truly she was sister to the three in *The Gleaners,* which once graced the wall of her stately country home.

"Entreat me not to leave thee. Whither thou goest, I will go." It was true of her and Gerhard. It was the unspoken song in Ruth Rosenbaum's heart. Christian Claassen hoped it was the song of Hedwig Wiehler's heart too, whenever fate and circumstance brought them face-to-face again.

Then, to add the final touches to the steaming gruel, Esther reached in her pocket. She drew out and tore into pieces the tops of the little green wild onions she had gathered at the roadside.

"Supper," she said, with thanksgiving in her heart.

Esther wondered when Ruth would be able to tell them about her life in the camp. They had heard ghastly whispers about the camps, but who could listen? Who did not turn away?

One evening after the family prayers, Ruth began to

talk. "I know that Germany despises the Russians, but they set us free. I would be dead by now had it not been for the Russian soldiers."

Ruth's huge eyes looked away, past the wallboards to a time and place where a part of her still lodged. She knew that it would take days, months, even years before a sufficient part of her was removed from that hell. "Who hath heard our report? To whom hath the arm of the Lord been revealed?"

"God reached out to the pits of hell, the stacks of frozen corpses, the famished ones fallen in the cold mud. He lifted me up."

Chris, ready to ask a question, leaned toward the Jewish girl.

He was stopped by Esther's hand on his thigh. "No, son, not now. Not now. Only what she wants to share."

Ruth's psyche and soul were stronger, though, than the Claassens realized. "Chaos reigned. When the commandant saw the country was overrun by the Russian tanks and soldiers, he fled with his sleek wife and his black-suited Nazi police.

"We were abandoned in the pits of hell. Even the furnaces were no longer burning. They couldn't keep up with all the dead and dying."

A huge tear slid down her sunken cheek. Eyes with the very soul of Jewish Rachael weeping for her children, looked upon them.

"The Kapos (camp guards) who managed the dead and the burnings became too weak to do their jobs. Besides, they were drunk, night and day. Who could blame them?

"I was pitched on a pile of corpses, unconscious. They dragged me from the dung-covered boards where we huddled. They thought I was dead. I only lost consciousness, not my life."

She looked at Christian. "Yes, the mercy of God was

with me, Christian. The love of the Jesus you people speak about. Love. Even in the pits of hell. Love."

Esther wiped her tears. Old Beulah began to sob and wail, "Blessed heart of Mary, blessed heart of Mary."

"I did not hear the rolling tanks or the Russian officer's commands, 'Find those still alive.' We had been told of the terrors from the Red hands, but even then, in those bloody hands, mercy prevailed for us.

"It took several days. Time was all the same. When I gained consciousness, I realized I was piled outside, along a wall. At first I said to myself, *I am dead, I am in Sheol.* Then my eyes began to focus. I tried to wiggle my fingers. Mercifully I found I was still alive."

Christian Claassen drew back at the horrors of the account. His mouth fell open. His heart ached.

"Somehow I managed to slide from the stack of cold corpses. I rolled and crawled through the mud of hades toward a clump of grass. I must give thanks for grass."

Something beyond Ruth had sustained her. She lifted her head. She was nearly bald from the camp shavings but the dark stubble meant dark hair would provide a covering for her head again.

Gerhard cleared his throat, eyes too full of tears to see across the room.

"When I could clear my head enough, and my eyes—" She faltered, for her soul had to take counsel with her body to see if it could continue.

"I saw the poor creatures tearing at the flesh of the dead. They seemed unaware. Sitting in the mud, tearing at the flesh of the dead. When they saw my eyes upon them, a hand stretched out, flesh in hand."

She tossed her head, as if tossing back those magnificent rippling locks at the side of her violin. The culture in her was still there but had gone underground for her survival.

186

"Thank the blessed God of Abraham for grass. Lying in the mud, I could reach the blessed grass. On that day I could still decide which blade of grass I would eat—this one or that."

Gerhard's sobs were the loudest, as they drew closer, their arms around one another.

"Oh, blessed broken heart of Mary. Oh, the crucified Jesus. Oh, oh!" wailed old homeless Beulah.

33

Next day, by afternoon, the sun had warmed the fields. Gerhard and Chris headed for the lane leading to farmer Max Wert's farm with hope in their hearts. With Gerhard's years of animal husbandry knowledge and skills, and with what Chris had learned from Gerhard, maybe Wert would make room for them. There was that empty tenant house in back of the farm. With a little repair, it could be made livable.

But Farmer Wert was in no mood for conversation. Who were these vagabonds from the east, overrunning his fields? A part of him soured with resentment. Let them glean, scrape, even dig for worms. How could things get back to normal on this farm, with hordes descending upon it like this?

But the fields yielded little, and Wert would not let them glean where the new crops were planted and leftover grains or roots might be found.

Gerhard ended up with only a small handful of barley grains, musty ones at that, in his sack. Chris had a few slices from rotten beets in his. Gloomily they decided to head back to the lane past the Wert house and plod home for another disappointing supper.

One of these days they would find work, real jobs. Hauling manure, milking cows—anything to get a toehold. Then the clock and watch shop for Gerhard. A dream, yes. But who knew? And Chris would go back to school. What was ahead for a young man after this war?

"Over here." Farmer Wert waved. He took his pipe from his mouth, shaking out the ashes. "Over here. That old house back there by the chicken house. Basement under it. Dead cow in the basement. God only knows how she fell in. Frozen in there all winter. Now with the May sun, she's gonna thaw. Blow our heads off. Gotta get her out."

They were used to dead animals—bloated horses; cows on their backs, bellies distended, black tongues rolling forward. They had even had to look at shreds of human beings in wire fences, not to mention the day of the trench and the Polish woman officer.

"Give you your supper. Get her out and I'll give you your supper. Don't suppose you got anything at all from that field yonder anyway. Real meat for supper, too."

It sounded too good to be true—meat, vegetables. Chris's mouth watered as visions of roast meat and potatoes flashed in his mind. He could even smell them. "Father, we can do it, we can do it."

They tried to keep up with Wert as he swaggered along the path to the weathered old house with the open basement windows.

"There she is. See for yourself."

But Chris and Gerhard didn't need to see for themselves. The cow had started to thaw. The stench almost blew their hats off.

Farmer Wert held his nose with his dirty-nailed fingers. "Get her out by five o'clock, and you're gonna have meat and vegetables enough for your family."

Chris turned at the crackling of a stick from a dried

limb along the path. Esther approached in the dress she had washed and patched that very morning.

"Thought I'd come out, get some air, and glean with you. The old ones and Ruth are resting." Then the overpowering odor from the basement hit her.

"Mercy, what is it? " The old terror filled her eyes. No. Not corpses. Surely they were past that now?

"Only a cow, Mother. A dead cow. Farmer Wert wants us to get her out of the basement she fell into. It'll take no time at all. No time at all. And he'll pay us with meat and vegetables for supper." Chris actually began to chuckle at their predicament.

"Then I'll help. I'm as strong as either of you." Esther, faded lavender rag-of-a-dress flapping around her thighs, headed for the opened stairwell and the gloom below it, putrefying smells or not. What was a little smell compared to a table spread with meat and potatoes?

Farmer Wert smirked. Suited them right, these peasants from the east. Looked Dutch, didn't they? Flat-headed Dutch. Should boil them some turnips and cabbage.

"Rope's down there. I pitched it in already. I'll be back later." He lumbered off, smirk still on his stubbly face.

Gerhard, eyes adjusting to the gloom, surveyed the situation. The cow was ten feet or so from the bottom of the concrete steps.

"Get the rope around her neck; it won't slide up past those horns. I see she's a Brown Swiss milk cow. Too bad a good cow like this had such misfortune."

Gerhard beckoned Chris to come ahead. He knelt on the cold dirt floor. His hands trembled slightly as he tried to make a noose and slip it over the head. The glazed eyes looked straight at him. The blackened tongue lolled forward.

"Let me, Father. I learned how to do all kinds of nooses and knots in the Jugend."

So Chris, hurrying with agile fingers, got the rope under the cow's head and neck, then pulled it taut.

"She'll be heavy, but we can do it. Mother, take hold here, Father, here. I'll take the end."

They stretched and pulled, their thin, empty-bellied bodies straining.

"Heave, heave, heave ho!" called Chris. "She's moving. She's moving."

But he'd strained so hard and leaned at such an angle, that his feet slid out from under him. He toppled to the cold floor. The sudden release on the rope made Esther and Gerhard topple.

They heaved. Their hearts knocked at their rib cages from the exertion.

"Whew. Whew." Gerhard was winded. "Whew, I don't know if we can move her that far." He eyed the afternoon sunlight through the opened cellar door.

"We can. Get up, Gerhard. Think of the meat and the potatoes." Esther didn't take time to think about *what kind* of meat it'd be. She hoped. She trusted.

It took them at least ten minutes of sweating and heaving, but they got the swollen cow halfway up the steps.

"Pull, pull, pull!"

Their thin hands, blistering now and sore from rope burns, slowly lost their grip on the tough, cutting rope.

The wild-eyed cow sank back to the bottom, emitting a "wooossh," as gas from the distended innards escaped.

"Now what? Do you think we should get her by the hindquarters, Gerhard?" Esther's dress was soiled with strange smears from contact with the thawing cow.

Just then farmer Wert leaned in at the top of the stairwell. "Ain't you folks done yet? I told you you'd have some supper when the job's done. May have to tell Ellie, my wife, to put that other kettle back off the fire." He disappeared.

"Try her by the hindquarters." Gerhard was determined. The cow's neck had unfortunately stretched too much. They couldn't get a firm hold on the animal. Her hindquarters would be more substantial, wouldn't slide down so easily.

But it turned out to be even tougher that way. There was more resistance, and her tail got in the way under her. More gas hissed out of the body.

Christian, not toughened by life as much as Esther and Gerhard, began to gag painfully.

They tried it six or seven times before they gave up. They needed a few minutes to rest and catch their breath. Esther took the lead. "We'll have to cut her up. Gerhard, isn't that an old ax with that hoe and sickle in the corner? "

Gerhard trembled from fatigue his shirt was drenched with sweat. He grasped the ax handle and began to swing.

"Father, just tell me where. I'll do it. I'm not as worn out as you. Let me have the ax."

Gerhard, having supervised butchering many a day, gave directions as if he were the butcher in the Schoensee meat market, preparing for the village banquet. "Her quarters, along here."

Chris swung. Chips of rotting flesh flew. This time Esther began to gag, but only for a moment. She remembered—supper awaited.

Farmer Wert appeared again. Diabolically he peered down into the gloomy hole. "Germany awake! What a smell. What are you doing? Not done yet?" He howled with laughter and was gone.

They tried not to think about what they gathered up, what portions; or how, in desperation, they tied them with the slimy rope. It was done. The task was done. Bloated pieces were piled by the dead maple tree. All three lay prostrate on the green spring grass, chests heaving, as the sun turned red in a western cloud bank.

"We did it." Chris whispered. "Mother, we did it."

"You want to come in and eat on the back porch? Ellie's got the supper ready. Bread and stew."

But Esther's stomach hadn't yet recovered from their revolting task. She doubted if Chris's or Gerhard's had either.

"If it's all the same to you, Mr. Wert, tell your kind wife, Ellie, to put our portion in a pail. We'll eat at . . ." She wanted to say "home," but it sounded ludicrous. Home? That corner in the dance hall, sleeping on moldy straw? Home?

Mrs. Wert put their portion in a pail. She generously ladled enough for six large servings, doubles at that. Esther saw carrots floating in the stew, potatoes, and maybe some parsnips. And meat. Bless God. Meat. Chunks of meat. Plenty of the chunks too. Give her a few moments more. She'd be able to face it by the time they walked "home."

They had to hold themselves back from swilling in gluttony. Chris hadn't dreamed horse meat could taste so good.

Gerhard slept little that night. The terrible exhaustion from his exertions with the cow had been too much. His hands and feet were cold in the dampness. His heart hammered. The fever rose again. He tossed, groaning on the straw.

Esther arose by the light of the moon through the window. She stoked the fire and put on some hot water, flavored with a few grains of the barley in her pocket.

Esther searched in her little pack for her remaining two aspirin. *Oh, merciful Father above*, she prayed, *did I hand them all over to Olga Fritzenheimer?*

She found two white tablets. They were not the same size or shape. Which was the one? She lifted his head; his silvery hair curled with sweat. "Gerhard, dear, I'll hold your head up. See if you can swallow these tablets. Chris, the water glass again."

He coughed, trying to swallow the tablets with such a swollen throat. His head sank into her lap.

"My good husband Gerhard. Soon we will have our place again. God knows. Soon. Soon." She mothered him as if he were a child in his mother's lap.

By the next evening, there was a late spring sprinkle of rain. Gerhard was worse. "My throat, Esther, my throat."

His rotten, rancid breath told of infection in his tonsils, organs that had given him trouble even in the Great War so long ago.

His fever raced. A doctor? What doctor? Where?

"Christian, I need help."

But Esther knew her words sounded helpless and feeble. Life depended on a source outside themselves. She turned her heart to prayer.

"Father, let me hold your head above the hard boards and the musty straw." Christian's young arms lifted his father's head and shoulders into his lap.

"I will talk to him until morning. Then maybe we can somehow find a doctor," he whispered, looking at his mother's fear-ridden face.

"Father? Awake? Morning will be here soon." The fever rose to life-threatening heights.

Gerhard opened his glassy eyes. "Christian, my son. My son. Is Hermann here too? Where is Esther?"

"I'm here beside you. Remember, we are safe. Ruth is here, Marie, Beulah. Think of our plans, Gerhard. The watch and clock shop. Maybe here in Damendorf. I'll help you. When you're better, I'll help you."

Gerhard opened his eyes and tried to lift his feverish head. "Yes. God saved us. Tomorrow, Christian, my son, my faithful son, you must take this chain." His trembling, hot fingers dragged a golden chain from his pocket.

"It is my father's watch chain, and, his father's before him. I want you and Hermann to have rings made from it. It comes from Danzig. It'll remind you of our home on the Werder."

His body shook from the chills alternating with the fever.

"The old way, Christian. Esther knows, she tells about it—the way. There's an old book somewhere . . ." He drifted into unconsciousness, fever still rising, throat red and swollen.

An easterly wind tore at the thin eaves of the building. Gerhard awakened again, still in the arms of his son.

"The sign was wrong, Chris. There is only one true sign. It is the cross." Chris knew that his beloved father meant the writhing, black cross of the swastika was the apostate one.

"Yes, father, I know." Tears ran down Chris's face. His father's parched lips whispered, a holy whisper. "Come, and let us return unto the Lord; for he hath torn, and he will heal us; he hath smitten, and he will bind us up."

Young tree branches brushed their only window. Planes, probably British, dropped bombs somewhere over east. Had the war ended? Were the Americans the victors? What was happening? Where would they settle?

Christian, new strength beginning slowly to surge through him, let the golden chain drop into his palm. His angular hand closed around it.

He wept. "Oh, Mother, no. Mother, no."

But it was death. Gerhard Claassen, of the Mennonites of the Werder, from Dutch ancestors, now a German in the dissolving Fatherland, was dead. He had died in the arms of his youngest son, named after the blessed Jesus himself —Christian.

34

Only the *Volksdeutsche*, those outside the borders of the Third Reich—the Polish and Russian German refugees—were eligible for assistance from the Fatherland. All others, the nationals, the *Reichsdeutsche* such as the Claassens, Ruth Rosenbaum, and Beulah Slavanski, were ineligible for aid. They'd have to scrounge on their own and seek a toehold wherever they could.

They had dropped spring flowers, buttercups, and daisies on Gerhard's grave in the little Lutheran cemetery across the way. Esther joined the company of the millions of grieving ones. In their little circle on the rude straw, her grief was shared by Ruth Rosenbaum, Beulah Slavanski, and Grandmother Froese, all bereaved.

She felt as though a two-mile chasm stretched before her. Yet she must cross it. Daily, step-by-step, she crawled down into the chasm of grief. Tumbling rocks, thorns, rushing waters. They, the grieving ones, must cross the chasm.

She did not unduly burden the family group with her private grief. Let the pain gnaw away at her heart in its own time. Chris needed her. Ruth, Grandmother, and Beulah needed her. And if they could find him, Hermann would need her. Where was there not a family broken, perishing in flight, destitute, and starving?

So, grieving but not despairing, Esther looked at Chris and smiled. She borrowed scissors from old Beulah, a tiny pair found at the bottom of her haversack.

"Don't cut it too short," said Christian, as the yellow hair fell to the floorboards. But he did admit, when he was in the washroom and looked at himself, that he looked cleaner. He was leaner, yes, and definitely tidier.

And bless God. Farmer Wert was so pleased with their work that ghastly afternoon that he had hired Chris as a hand on the farm.

Esther and Chris counted the two deutsche marks he'd earned thus far. "In a couple of weeks, Mother. Start looking, start looking."

And she did. Esther walked the streets of Damendorf. "A little apartment above a bakery. I think we'll be able to afford it, Chris. And Ruth is gaining strength each day. She's checking to see if anyone will loan her a violin so, when we're settled, she can earn money by giving lessons. Beulah can keep house if I get a job in the bakery. She can watch over Grandmother Froese."

Arthur Krahn, who had been hired on at the freight yard to unload coal, came by just in time to meet Chris loping home from his farm chores. "Explore the town tonight? Bombings have stopped. For all practical purposes, the war is over."

They hadn't gotten used to saying it yet—"The Allies have won." In time. Still, they were young and alive and life beckoned them.

"Sure, Art. After our supper, come by. We'll take a walk together in Damendorf."

How could Esther say no to her boy, now a young man? She wanted to forbid him, but she was wise enough to know that they had crossed a watershed. Gradually she must step back so that he could discover who he was and where he wanted to go. War quickly drained the adolescence from the youth.

The night life was surprising. Lights were flashing again over the taverns. Bombings had stopped. The whole world knew that in faraway Warm Springs, Georgia, President Roosevelt of the United States of America had died on April 12, 1945.

Herr Hitler and his famous henchmen, Herr Goebbels, Herr Goering, and Herr Himmler—designer of the ghastly ovens and concentration camps—had met for their "last party."

To the end, the Führer, the inventor of the famous flag with the Black Spider, ranted and raved. He seemed to be completely insane. "Traitors! Cowards! You have deserted me! You brought it on. Traitors!"

On April 29, 1945, Hitler and Eva Braun were married in a short ceremony. On April 30, 1945, one of the most infamous dictators the world had known, along with his bride, reportedly committed suicide.

Cobblestones shone purple, pink, and red in front of the Weisse Stein, a restaurant and tavern which was surprisingly crowded. Enthralled by the merriment and the raucous, joyful engagements of men and women beyond the window, the two youths in their faded clothing stood peering through the glass.

"Soon, Chris, we'll have money enough to bring our mothers here for supper. Soon." Though he had eaten black bread and porridge for supper, Arthur's mouth watered as waiters in white aprons set food—actual meat upon plates—and beer before the patrons.

"Who's that?" Arthur pressed his nose to the glass. No. It couldn't be. A tall girl, red lips open in laughter, tilted her head and tossed her black hair as she lifted her stein.

"Hedwig? Chris, is that Hedwig Wiehler?"

Nose to the glass beside Arthur, Chris focused his eyes. No. It couldn't be. "Yes, it is! Art, that *is* Hedwig Wiehler sitting there."

Chris's heart pounded. His knees trembled as he reached for the door handle. "Art, Art. Oh, God above, my prayers have been answered."

At first the laughing girl seated on a bentwood cafe chair didn't notice the two lanky, starved-looking, disheveled young men. Her darkened eyebrows raised as she reached for her beer stein, bewildered. But what could one expect these days? The country was overrun with vagabonds. An empty plate and beer stein sat opposite her. She placed her smoking cigarette on the edge of the ashtray.

Chris tried not to bolt to her side, but in his haste he bumped a chair. Heads turned.

"Hedwig. Hedwig." He had uttered her name too loudly. All eyes focused on the boy with the funny haircut sidling up to the table where the beauty sat.

"Oh, my God, Hedwig. I thought you went down on the *Riefenstahl*. At last. Hedwig—" His arm reached out awkwardly to take her hand.

She drew back—hand, arm, shoulders, chin, all. She tossed her head. "Chris? Chris Claassen? Chris Claassen of the Grosse Werder? Well, it is. I see you made it." Her matter-of-fact words spilling from her painted lips carried little warmth or surprise.

Chris reached again for her hand, forgetting the onlookers, not noticing that there was a definite pull of her arm against the tug of his hand.

"Hedwig, how did you make it? Where—how—?"

Obviously the young man was befuddled, making more of an event than he should. That was the way with refugees, always overreacting. He talked loudly, like a wild-eyed country bumpkin.

Arthur Krahn stood by, shifting his feet in embarrassment as Chris tried to cope with this surprising reality.

Just then, the second chair was drawn back by a man clothed in a military uniform. A young lieutenant in the British Air Force looked at Hedwig. "These young men your brothers?" His eyes ran up and down the lanky forms of the youths in patched, baggy trousers with more than a hint of manure on them.

"Just someone I met on the journey here, Jerry. Just new acquaintances made a short time ago. One meets so many refugees these days, you know." She said it disdainfully. After all, why tell the whole story when you've snagged a lieutenant—on the victor's side, too.

She picked up her cigarette, enclosing the tip with her red lips, and blew the smoke toward Christian. "Same old name, huh? We talked about getting you another name, didn't we?" A rippling chuckle shook her shoulders and hair.

"Hedwig, how could you? After our—" Chris Claassen's heart pounded. Words rattled in his confused mind. His tongue tangled. Nothing seemed clear. The whole world was upside down.

"Jerry Rockford here, Lieutenant Jerry Rockford. And you?" The handsome officer towered before him.

"Uh, oh, Claassen. Christian Claassen," he stammered. He was going to say, "Of the Werder, the Gross-Werder," but a part of him held back, realizing how backwoods it sounded. His heart knocked against his ribs. Arthur Krahn looked on, aching for his friend.

"A table, sirs?" a waiter asked. His words spilled out scornfully. Another pair with not a penny for a tip. Hardly even a coin for a beer.

"The lieutenant and I have been together for two months now, Chris. And," she glanced at Arthur, "I've forgotten his name."

She rose from her chair, her skirt swishing around her silk-stockinged calves. "By the way, could you two boys check to see if either of your mothers are going to be taking in washing. Let me know."

She reached her red-nailed hand across to the lieutenant with the broad shoulders and angular jaw. "Come, Jerry, we'll be late for the concert." Hedwig tipped her head regally, and she and the lieutenant walked to the door.

"Well, I hope you boys get a job on a farm somewhere," she called back, stepping high to keep pace with the handsome lieutenant striding triumphantly down the walk.

Now Chris had his own chasm. The grief over his father, yes—but now his first love. The things they had shared, the loving embraces of young bodies, the sweet whisperings and promises amidst bombs and shells bursting—did it really mean nothing to Hedwig?

That night Chris buried his head in the moldy straw on the hard boards, too embarrassed to cry and too ashamed to tell Esther.

35

Surprising how real linoleum on the floor and counter in the tiny kitchen boosted Esther's heart. These last few mornings, up at five o'clock to put the kettle on, she caught herself humming and singing, "Now thank we all our God."

They had partitioned the small bedroom, dividing it into three sleeping areas. No one had a bed yet. But give them time. Scrounging for old draperies and sheets, Chris strung the wires, making separate "bedrooms."

Chris took the tiny enclosure by the door. Grandmother Froese and Beulah took the third to the left. That left the small west portion for Esther and Ruth. Already Chris had brought home two abandoned chairs—broken, yes, but he had skillfully wired them together. Chairs! Esther began to feel civilized again.

Chimes announcing morning lauds gently wafted through the half-opened kitchen window. A sound of civilization, a church somewhere. It must be St. Mary's Catholic.

She poured the scalding water over the tea leaves in her cup, inhaling the fresh fragrance. Tea. No more strange brownish swill they had called coffee. She savored it, the cup warming her hands.

"Morning, Mother."

"Chris. You could have slept longer. You've been working so hard." Her hazel eyes focused on his tall frame. No, he hadn't gained weight yet; it worried her. A growing boy needed good food, meat, potatoes, milk.

"Max Wert's asked me to take charge of his dairy cows. Means I should get there earlier this morning. We're making it, Mother. When he pays me again, we can buy some mattresses and maybe a table."

Chris' smile showed his even white teeth. His blue eyes reflected an innocence triumphing over his own pain.

After his tea, drunk from a cracked cup, and the two slices of thick brown bread Esther brought home from the bakery, he was on his way. He had leather shoes on his feet. Used ones, given out by the Relief Society, but he didn't have to clop through manure in wooden shoes. Whew! What a splash that made!

By seven o'clock that evening, he was back at the tiny apartment above the bakery on Tillenstrasse, an old, backward street, but a street nevertheless. Aging brick and stone houses with blackened chimneys and tile roofs were two or three stories high. Old, shabby—but home for now. And, Chris smiled to himself, they had an address, and this week the postman had started delivering mail.

Well, nothing for the Claassens, or for Grandmother, or for old Beulah, or for Ruth Rosenbaum yet. Give it time. They would make their scratch on the earth deep enough to be noticed. Give them time.

And Ruth? How graceful she was beginning to look. Her complexion was still clear, although her eyes were filled with the sadness of a lost river seeking its outlet. Her hair, now growing out, curled softly on her lifted head. Her eyes had brightened last evening when she actually came up the stairs without holding the railing all the way.

"Chris, Esther. Oh, good fortune! Reverend Honecker of the Lutheran Church across the way has an old violin. He said he would restring it and have it ready for me tomorrow." She had almost smiled.

Soon. Give her time. Stutthof was not left behind in a day. And Ruth had not told all of her experiences. Some things need much time before they may be told. And even then the victims may be disbelieved by the horror-stricken and denying hearers.

Chris couldn't remember such pride on his mother's face since they left the Werder. She looked marvelous in her white apron over the clean if faded lavender dress that surprised them all and still hung together at the seams.

"A letter, Christian Claassen, addressed to Christian Claassen, this number in Damendorf." Wrinkles showed around her eyes as her lips spread in happiness.

"It's from America. Kansas. From Whitewater, Kansas. Uncle Peter Penner. You remember his visit, before the —?"

Chris held the slightly soiled envelope. He couldn't believe it. The only mail he'd received since long ago, since the last of the Hitler Youth mailings announcing their meetings and their endeavors.

"A knife, Mother, a knife." It wouldn't do to rip open such a letter with a clumsy finger, a soiled one at that.

She handed him the small paring knife.

The two crisp pages unfolded in Chris's unwashed hands.

"Oh, I should have washed my hands." Such a momentous event, yet here he was holding the precious pages with soiled hands.

"Read it, Chris. Read it." She tossed her silvery head; her hazel eyes filled with wonder. "What does it say?"

Oh, blessed letter. It had not sunk to the bottom of the Atlantic as did millions of others, in torpedoed ships.

"My Dear Nephew Christian." There it was on the page, his name. He was someone, someone on the earth, someone who was important enough for this. It was amazing. No longer a refugee but a real person, a citizen who received letters. Letters from that heavenly place, the United States of America. Forget what the Führer said about it. Chris had long ago admitted that the Führer hadn't known it all.

"Read it out loud. Read it!" Esther had to sit down on one of the wired-together chairs.

"I'm enclosing ship passage on the *Titus*, which is leaving on the Rhine from Dusseldorf. I have the agreement of the Immigration Services of the United States to be your sponsor.

"By now you are a young man. The farm here is large, more than a thousand acres. We can use your help. This is a large Mennonite community . . ."

"There is a God who hears our prayers." Esther sagged on the chair. "America. America." Her hazel eyes were filled with wonder, unbelievable wonder that her son, her very own Christian was invited to such a haven. She stood up and embraced him.

Then it struck her. Yes. Yes. She would let him go. Yes, God above, yes.

And as she held his lithe, warm body, smelling faintly of barnyard manure, she ran her calloused fingers through his straggly hair. "My boy. My boy. Christian, my little Mennonite boy of the Werder."

And Esther Claassen broke into sobs, heaving sobs, as she began to realize what it actually would mean.

Christian saw flat land. Dust, and hundreds and hundreds of acres of wheat. Uncle Peter and Aunt Hester and too many other Mennonites ever to count were here in Kansas, a state with sunflowers, heat, and scalding sun.

There was wind, wind, wind, like that of the Werder, with the fall northwesters blowing the waves over the dikes.

And the food—the Mennonite sausages, the borscht, and all the other Russian foods these "Russian" Germans brought to this land. Who could believe how easy it was to get a toehold in America?

"Coming up the Mississippi to New Orleans, seeing those little poles and sticks holding up the shacks along the great river, I thought I was in Africa," Chris had announced bashfully, after all the *Verwandtschaft* (relatives) had embraced him, the women wetting his cheek with kisses.

But he had settled in. America. He had to learn English quickly, had to force himself to speak English. Here in Whitewater folks all spoke German, like back at Ladekopp Mennonite Church on the Werder. But Chris knew he would not live in Whitewater forever.

He had been with Uncle Peter less than a year. He had enjoyed learning to know the girls of the community who flashed smiles at him. Then the news broke: "United States at War in Korea."

Should he go back to Germany? Maybe never get back to the United States with the churches, the people, the cars, cars, cars? The abundance, the squandering, the throwing away, the movies, the—?

While the Kansas wind howled at the eaves of his bedroom, Chris tossed. His muscles had been hardened by the drudgery. He had wrestled the mammoth tractor over the hard ground, ripping it open with a half-dozen plows. He had helped with the milking of the forty Holsteins. He remembered combining wheat, combining, combining, combining forever. It was like that account in Scripture about young Jacob wrestling with an angel. The agony of it, the all-night turnings of it. He couldn't stop the words that raced through his mind, as he could not stop the howling of the Kansas wind at the eaves.

"There is a way which seemeth right unto a man, but the end thereof are the ways of death."

He turned. The wind calmed down, then picked up speed again.

The words rolled. "But I say unto you . . . Love your enemies, do good to them which hate you. Bless them that curse you and pray for them which despitefully use you."

On the second night of Christian Claassen's tossings in the stark upstairs bedroom, the old nightmare engulfed him. A thousand banners encircled him. Not banners, flags that whipped out to drag him into the center of the circle.

Chris could hear himself talking: "Oh, the Black Spider."

The swastika flags dipped and leaped forward. Then the old traumatic ending. The center of the Spider swelled with blood. Its eyes opened and the red mouth, dripping with blood smiled and called his name, "Chris, Christian, of the Werder. It is we, the Führer and the Fatherland. We command your all. Chris, Chris. . . ."

The ghostly voice echoed in his ears as Chris awoke, choking back a scream, his body dripping with sweat. He sat up on the edge of the bed to regain his composure. He turned on the lamp, picked up the tattered New Testament, and began to read from the Gospel of Luke.

This time the crisp, hardly soiled letter was for Esther. And it was addressed properly to 24 West Lindenstrasse. This was a better district. They had a newer, three-room apartment with a rug on the floor, a gleaming bathroom, a view of a small park, and still the chimes from a church.

Esther kissed the letter from her boy of the Werder before she opened it. Esther used the letter opener to slice carefully, with care and love. A message from Chris. Messages from sons to mothers border on the holy.

"Dearest Mother." Her eyes raced. Esther had to sit down in her second-hand rocker. Her heart palpitated. A weakness crept up her legs.

"Here in America, Mother, there is conscientious objection provided for those who by conscience cannot go to war. The old confession of our church inspired me, as I struggled to work it through.

"The United States is at war in Korea. I have registered, Mother, as a conscientious objector to war. I chose to follow the example set by our Lord, and the instruction that he gave in St. Luke."

The pages fell from her hands. Tears flowed down a face now wrinkled and seasoned by trials. "Oh, my son. Christian, you have vindicated us. You have chosen the best part. The seeds of our holy confession bore fruit."

Esther's heart warmed with the same glow she used to feel singing at Ladekopp church. She hadn't noticed that she had begun to rock. She was not even conscious that she was singing the same hymn that she and old Grandmother Froese had sung on the whaling ship when Grandfather died.

> Jesus still lead on, till our rest be won,
> and although the way be cheerless,
> We will follow, calm and fearless;
> guide us by thy hand to our fatherland.

The rocking soon ceased, as tired old Esther Claassen, long ago of the Werder Mennonites, drifted off in a blissful sleep.

36

It hadn't seemed long at all, the way the years slid by. Some clustered around signposts along the way—funerals, weddings, births, baptisms, graduations, anniversaries.

It had seemed too much at first for Hermann, reluctant as he was after his imprisonment in the British prisoner of war camp north of Düsseldorf. "There was brutality and starvation. The British had a lot of hatred for us Germans. Can't say I blame them, considering it all, but then . . ."

There had been much suffering and early death. Hermann, however, hung on. His limp and his slightly lowered left shoulder were the tokens of his service.

"I remember the day you knocked on the apartment door. You were out of breath from climbing the steps, just as I was for months after release from Stutthof." Ruth looked at her husband with soulful brown eyes.

"I said, 'Well now, there's a pair of us,' both of us thin as worn-out britches on a clothesline."

Ruth reached for his shoulders, looking into his dark eyes. "It will be a blessing, Hermann, to have our family together again, even for a brief visit. Your mother's not going to live forever. Eightieth birthday."

Ruth Rosenbaum Claassen stared at the oil portrait of Esther Froese Claassen, hanging on the silk burgundy paper, her silver hair still regal. Esther, a good name for this woman.

Ruth glanced again at her husband, a little hunch shouldered, yet tall and dignified. He was more of the silent type since the war, with no more bragging about Nuremberg. He looked the other way or left the room when news of the Hitler era came on the television screen. They buried so much, these German soldiers.

Who would have believed their progress, their accomplishments? She was professor of string music at the University of Düsseldorf. He had an office in one of those dark glass towers as an accountant for top German megacompanies.

Christians, yes. Her Jewishness provided the backdrop. As her kindly father, God rest his soul, had always reminded her, "Jesus was a Jew."

She and Hermann were members in St. Anthony's Lutheran Church over west in Düsseldorf. They, as most Germans, attended on high days, Christmas, and Easter.

Their fifteen-year-old son, Eric, had been baptized as an infant and was a member of the church. But like most adolescent European boys nowadays, he was a bit agnostic, a bit confused. Today Mick Jagger, tomorrow . . ? Maybe blue denim, long hair, Harley Davidson T-shirt and a black leather jacket proclaiming "rebel" and "wild one."

Hermann's hands, clasped his thin, dark wife. She was a wife of great beauty. "I love you, Ruth. The first time I saw you I knew it. It was when you played the violin and that woman, the maid Olga, blasted us all in the name of the—" But he didn't say it, that last word. It would cause his tongue to tangle, his jaw to ache.

They sat together on the rich brocade of the couch. Never had they dreamed in the old days that they'd sit on cloth like this again, in a room like this, in a nine-room apartment in the finest area of Düsseldorf.

Hermann would be drawn almost into ecstasy as he'd stand, warm hand on Ruth's shoulder, while she played Mendelssohn on the grand piano in the sunny bay windows by the exotic plants.

Eric's music? It bombed his brain. He needed to take time one of these days to sit down with Eric and get it sorted out. At least he hoped he could. But who could understand those lyrics? Hermann and Christian had had their symbols in their day. Father Gerhard listened but never made much comment. Mother was genteel. They knew she was addicted to classical music, and, of course, the hymns of the church. Yes, Christian and Hermann had had their marching music. Not rock, but heavy-booted marching music to build the calf muscles.

"When will Chris and Mara arrive in Danzig? Have you received anything from them yet?" Hermann wanted to be sure that lodging for the Claassen family was secured at the Danzig *Novotel* on the Pszenna. A good hotel, secure. Security mattered. Mother was getting older and he wanted to provide the best for her. He called ahead to reserve a sizable van, roomy enough to carry them all out to the old Gross-Werder. A part of him, deep inside, was still reluctant, actually nervous.

He wondered what the village of Schönsee looked like now. How had the four "collective farm" families done on their farm? Had the eleven-room house with attached barn survived the ravages of time? The wear of Polish families through the years? It would be nice if that old Polish-German woman, Beulah Slavanski, were alive to go back with them. But she had passed on only two years after Mother Claassen started working at that bakery. Beulah had been buried in Catholic style.

The carved ivory door to the apartment opened. Eric

strolled in and slammed the door. Somewhere chimes sounded in the apartment. He had returned from his schoolmate Willie's apartment, ears ringing from listening to heavy metal.

Wonder what Eric's identity is this month? said Hermann to himself. Their son was brilliant. He attended the best prep school in Düsseldorf, where he studied advanced sciences and math. Yet why was it that for the adolescent their accomplishments, his and Ruth's, their books, their concerts, and their music had to be "all wrong"?

For the past two months, Eric had been dressing in rock star getup. It bothered Hermann a lot. He knew Grandmother Esther wouldn't understand, but she wouldn't say anything. She would only smile at the boy, reassuring Hermann, "Give him time, give him time."

Eric was dark like his mother Ruth. He was destined for a brilliant scientific career, they had been told by the school headmaster, provided he didn't get sidetracked on some minor issue. "Your boy is brilliant, but it may be a tussle to keep him at his studies."

But, thought both Hermann and Ruth, who wasn't confused about how and what role to live these days? Besides, according to the best psychologists, adolescence was a stage of trying on various hats, seeing which personality fit. They had provided a few sessions with the eminent psychiatrist, Dr. Solon Rittenhouse, but the boy was so uncooperative they gave up.

"Too much pressure on adolescents nowadays," said Hermann. "Grandmother is right, give him time."

Eric growled at his father and headed toward his spacious room, newly decorated this spring. He planned to get some banners, flags, maybe posters to add to the decor on his east wall. What was it Dad once decorated his wall with? Deutsche marks? How common.

Slouching in an expensive teakwood chair in the bay

window of the room, Eric sorted through his mail. What was this? He opened a fat envelope of cheap paper and pulled out the small pamphlet.

"Well, isn't this interesting, war memorabilia." His heart picked up a beat as he began to leaf through the pamphlet. He hadn't yet read the letter, which had been personally addressed to him. The unmarked envelope contained materials from the New German Aryan Society.

Then his mother called. A big part of him wished he didn't have to go to Gdansk for a family reunion. Americans were such bores. So blasé, so out of touch with issues now involving the world.

But he loved Grandmother Claassen, except he didn't really believe some of her old stories. Her mind was surely going. There was a name for it, but he couldn't get it on his tongue just now.

Christian Claassen from the state of Kansas disembarked from the jumbo jet, his wife, Mara Helmuth Claassen, behind him.

She looked over her shoulder, unaware that she copied something from a prior era—"the German look." She was apprehensive at being behind the iron curtain. "Will we be safe?" Thoughts of Stalinist soldiers, Red guards, Nazi troops, and the word *Hitler* frightened her.

Nevertheless, she looked calm as she followed Chris. She was dressed simply, according to the precepts of Mennonites, particularly those from her home area in the eastern United States.

When Christian read that chapter in Luke about doing good to one's enemies, he read other parts of the New Testament too. He became a committed Mennonite. He and Mara pledged themselves wholly to the old ways, to the ways waning even in the United States as acculturation took its toll.

"Matthew, are you keeping up?" Mara turned, suitcase dragging one arm down, to check on her fourteen-year-old son. He was stumbling along with his own overstuffed cloth bag.

Matthew, heart beating from the excitement of coming at last to Grandmother's country, tossed his head. His hair, hair like his father used to have, fell to the side.

"Mother, I can't believe we are here. Can't believe it." His intense eyes focused on the glass front of the airport exit to the waiting taxis.

"Dad, such a big city." Like Philadelphia. Bigger than Kansas City. He was eager to meet his German cousin, Eric Claassen.

"Kansas City is a river-shipping and railroad distribution center. Danzig—or Gdansk as it's now called—is a major seaport on the Baltic. It was a site of infighting between the Polish and Germans in my time."

Christian turned, putting his arm around his struggling son. He was worried. Mara looked terrified when she saw the officials in their navy uniforms and military-style caps, with stern looks on their faces. The sign above read "Immigration and Passports."

Old fears caused Chris's back to chill. He shifted his foot nervously, handing the passports to the tallest officer. An old scar on his thigh began to throb. Some of the old feelings were coming back.

"Onward, ahead." The nearly rude officer handed back their passports and waved them through the turnstile.

They were permitted to pass. Thank God! Chris hadn't allowed for emotions such as these. His forehead glistened with sweat.

A blue-suited airport attendant ushered them to a waiting taxi. Mara scanned the skyline with its new buildings. Old towers of churches and the town hall had been restored after the German bombings. Tradition—that was it.

Europe had tradition, plus a history of endless wars.

"What is that?" Mara grabbed Christian's arm, pointing east.

"That's Artus Hall, destroyed by German bombings but rebuilt after the war. Ought to be the tower of St. Mary's church around here too. We used to have appointments at Ruth's father's office somewhere around here. Doctor Rosenbaum. A fine, fine man. But he perished in Auschwitz." His voice was edged with sadness. The pain clawed at his chest. He hadn't calculated how heavy and choking it would feel.

These were things Mara didn't ask about. The war, the Hitler Youth, the Nazis, the terrible trek, and sufferings of getting out of the country. She was wise enough to wait for Christian to share in his own time. Bit by bit, she'd learned some of his history. She knew there were parts of it that he would tell no one.

Well, he did tell young Matthew a story of an indescribable afternoon trying to get some kind of dead animal out of a basement. She remembered that!

They drove past grim houses, medieval buildings mixed in with the new. Red trolley cars hummed and wobbled along on their shiny rails. Christian hoped it didn't rain. He knew his mother would want the skies clear, the sun bright. Besides, the old road out of Schoensee might still be dirt.

Hermann had called before they left Kansas, explaining that he, Ruth, and their son, Eric, would be arriving with mother by five-thirty or six. That would give him and his family time to check in at the Novotel, freshen up, and get their bearings. Christian wanted Matthew and Mara to be in the lobby when his mother and brother and his family came through the imposing hotel doors.

Actually, Esther had been to Newton, Kansas, twice to

visit them. "Reminded me of the Gross-Werder," she had said, "Only if it'd rained more. The flat land, the wind."

She'd be considerably older now. Eighty? Fragile, maybe, but not feeble. No, he could not imagine Esther Claassen feeble, not even in her old age.

She was the first to come through the glass and brass revolving door. The silver-headed grandmother with hair in a French twist was stately, She wore a long-sleeved rose shirtwaist dress which accented her still lean, tall frame.

Her lined face spread in a happy smile. "Christian. Christian. I can't believe you're here. And Mara." Esther kissed one then the other with motherly exuberance.

"And look at Matthew." She drew the smiling adolescent close to her, embracing him. "Matthew, Matthew. Oh, you remind me so of your father when he was fourteen."

The brothers dropped their bags, shook hands, and embraced. Ruth and Mara exchanged kisses and hugs. The adolescent boys looked at each other uncomfortably for a moment, then shook hands. Matthew's eyes widened at the sight of Eric's punk hair and costume. He himself would like to experiment more, but the boundaries were tight in Newton, Kansas. He didn't want to be hooted out of town.

He would learn a lot from his cousin, he thought. Give them time to break the ice. Why did his parents have to be so conservative, anyway? Nevertheless, Matthew shared his family's enthusiasm for making contact with old family lands and roots.

37

Bright sunlight spilled down from the morning sky. The dark green van rolled smoothly on the macadam expressway which stretched beyond suburban Gdansk to the old Gross-Werder.

Esther, in front with Hermann at the wheel, clasped her purse with long, work-worn fingers. Her eyes were wide with anticipation. She had checked to see if she had her handkerchief. She knew there would be tears, plenty of tears. But smiles too. What had Solomon written? "A time and a season for everything."

"Neunhuben coming up. Boys, it was once a center of Mennonites. It's called *Diewiet Wlok* now."

All eyes focused across the flat lowlands, green pastures, rows and rows of new sugar beet plants, and willow-lined drainage ditches dug at regular intervals.

"I want to see a windmill," said Matthew. He was in the back of the van with his cousin, Eric, who had been on this tour once before with his father.

Eric hoped he could cope with the boredom. Nevertheless, cousin Matt was no dullard. He seemed open to new ideas. *Don't write him off yet*, thought Eric, glancing at his American cousin's traditional haircut. They hadn't had time to talk about sex yet. Eric would bring him up to date, liven things up. Maybe give him some lessons. Americans were surely backward on that subject. Then too, Eric wanted to ask Matt about that group out in Washington state, the *Brüder Schwergen*, the Silent Brotherhood. Too bad he hadn't had time to read the materials in the envelope that had arrived just before he had to leave for this excursion.

Once in a while gracious old trees, lindens and poplars, framed elegant old mansions along the road. Whoever built them had money and had made a statement. Some were well preserved, two-storied, with arcaded fronts with pillars so carriages and cars could drive through.

"The richer Mennonites built many of those old homes. Now, of course, near Schoensee, houses like those, even our old farmhouse, make a home for a collective farm group of five or six families sometimes." Christian's face sobered as his mind remembered the old losses.

Their first stop was in Schönsee. It was still a village. The town hall was still there. How tiny. There were quaint cobblestone streets and ramshackle shops.

Christian's heart missed a beat. His color paled as momentarily a ghastly memory flashed through his mind: six male bodies swinging by their necks under the sign, "They were traitors to the Reich." Kettle drums roared in his head for a moment. He wondered if he would be sick. When he opened his eyes, he more than half-expected to see an ugly flag thrusting toward them in the wind, mockingly, the Black Spider reaching out.

"Are you all right?" Mara took his hand.

"I'm all right, Mara. It's just . . . the power of it, the images returning."

Esther Claassen tightened her hold on her lace-edged handkerchief, unaware that her body tensed. She leaned forward. "Stop, Hermann. Stop. I want to get out and walk about."

Ruth said, "I remember the day we rolled through this street in the buggy. I was a young Jewish girl from the city. My violin was in Christian's arms. You held me, Mother Claassen. You held me, and I knew you were praying." Ruth's eyes widened as her fine-boned hand caressed her throat.

"You prayed too, my child. I can hear your prayer when you last laid eyes on your dear father. 'Shema, Israel; Hear O Israel, the Lord our God is one.' " Tears glistened in Esther's eyes.

Christian and Hermann strolled down past St. Matthew Lutheran church. How dingy, how small. But it had survived. The bell tower was gone.

"Our church was outside the village." Esther felt a chill, but her arm was steady as she pointed toward the road leading to the farm. She wanted to rush there. Yet along with the happy memories weaving through the fabric of her very life was the terrible pain—those other memories.

They were silent as they gathered where the Ladekopp Mennonite church once stood. A few Holstein cows rested under a linden tree. In the cemetery some headstones had fallen into the grass. Others were still standing but tilted.

"Listen to the wind," said Esther.

"It is almost as if the wind carries their names."

She only whispered the family names, tears sliding down her parchment face: "Andres, Brucks, Dirksen, Entz, Epp, Loewen, Thiessen . . ."

Hermann stepped to his mother's side. He put his arm around her waist as Ruth took her hand and began to speak. "I learned something here. Here in this church, I learned that the God of you Christians is the God of Israel. I shall never forget that hymn, 'Holy God, We Praise Thy Name.' I, a forlorn refugee girl, named Ruth Swartzentruber, was comforted by that song."

"Oh, that we had followed the holy God more faithfully." Christian only whispered the words. They were more his prayer. He had no intention of making anyone feel guilt.

"When Father died in our arms, Mother, remember what he said?" asked Christian.

"Yes, son, he told us the flag was wrong. We all knew it; it was buried somewhere within."

Hermann coughed to cover the crest of emotion in his chest. He said, "So much seemed so good at first. When Hitler annexed the Danzig Free State to Germany, our markets increased, prices skyrocketed. It was a new day for us. Hitler wanted to preserve family farms. All farms were to stay in the families, going to the youngest son. Chris, that would have been you."

Herman could have gone on. He knew the struggles of the German peoples against the hated Versailles Treaty, the unfair reparations demanded by the victors in World War I, which brought about mass German unemployment and misery.

"Would it be all right if I read something from the Bible?" Esther smiled at her brood. She avoided overzealous religiosity. Nevertheless she was standing on holy ground. God only knew what would again come forth from this ground of the Werder. Hadn't some old prophet written, "From the bitter came forth the sweet"?

They smiled at her. "Read, Mother, whatever you want."

Esther's hands trembled, no longer searching for a rolling pin but for a small Bible in her purse. Straining, her old hazel eyes focused on the words from Leviticus 26:3-4, 6. "If ye walk in my statutes, and keep my commandments, and do them; Then I will give you rain in due season, and the land shall yield her increase, and the trees of the field shall yield their fruit. . . . And I will give peace in the land,

and ye shall lie down, and none shall make you afraid."

Ruth Rosenbaum Claassen wept openly. "Oh, Mother Claassen, my father, my beloved father used to recite it in the synagogue. 'None shall make you afraid.' "

Matthew Claassen swallowed a lump in his throat. Yes, he knew about Hitler. He knew about Mennonites, especially in America. But until now he had not quite realized that the two had contended with each other. He remembered his father, far-off look in his eye, once telling him, " I used to call the swastika the Black Spider over Tiegenhof."

Then too, his dad had been a conscientious objector during the Korean War. Would he himself ever have to really face that issue, being drafted? Why did he feel so unsettled just now? He looked at his cousin, Eric. But Eric was tossing a few stones across the road ditch to a startled flock of crows. He didn't seem as moved by a visit to old ruins. Matthew Claassen wondered how Eric got his Mohawk hair style to stand up like it did. He'd have to ask him when they got back to the hotel.

38

Hermann Claassen steered the van down the lane toward the old Dutch farmhouse. The house and attached barn were still standing. Cedar, hemlock, and linden trees towered around it. The lawn was overgrown in spots, bare in others. Piles of rubbish were strewn near the back of the house.

"Old Beulah's cottage." Ruth pointed to the pile of stones and elderberry bushes along the land. Her hand gripped her throat again. "This is where they came and took me. Oh, God."

Esther reached back, taking Ruth's hand in hers.

Hermann and Chris stepped from the van as a heavy woman, black kerchief covering her head, turned from the leaning clothesline. A small group of dark-clothed women and children raked through Esther's once beautiful garden. They leaned on hoes apprehensively, looking toward the stranger.

"Oh, Grandmother, is this where you once lived, and Dad too?" Matthew felt the pull of his European roots.

His mother, Mara, was silent, almost too silent. The whole excursion bordered on the holy for her. Family was important. Even though she was nervous, she was at the same time thankful. Glad for Christian.

Two Polish men dragging scythes ambled around the corner of the barn where Christian played as a boy. Ahead he could see the willows drooping by the pond where had sat with Ruth long ago.

"Greetings," the older man nodded, his heavy farmer's cap pulled slightly over his forehead. They approached hesitantly.

The younger man, more hunch-shouldered from bending, nodded, his face stern. Esther saw that after an exchange of a few words they shook hands with her sons, then nodded. There were no smiles. None. A chill wind blew over the Werder. The sun momentarily hid behind a cloud. What had the Black Spider wrought? And then the hammer and the sickle?

Christian beckoned with his arm, calling, "Come, Mother, Matthew, Ruth, all of you. The head man of the collective has given us permission to go through the house."

Christian nodded his thanks to the farmers leaning against the doorframe of the barn. An empty longing marked their faces.

Esther Claassen trembled visibly now. She reached for Mara and Ruth, standing between them. "Oh, my daughters, I can scarcely endure it."

Broken boards met her foot on the once beautiful veranda. Rags hung in the bay window where her piano had stood, where Ruth had played her violin one fearful night.

Above their heads bare light bulbs hung from the ceilings. They replaced the beautiful fixtures which had been sold by the collective administrators who had divided the rooms and pocketed the money.

It took old Esther a while to get her bearings. Her long gloved fingers brushed at a wisp of gray hair at her brow. Yet a smile touched her lips.

Then she said, "Christian, what is it? It doesn't seem . . ."

"No, Mother, it's changed. The walls. Don't you see? Four families live here. It has been divided."

In a tumbled bed in the corner, a sick child lifted its head and began to cry for its mother.

"The stove. Yes, my stove." The giant kitchen range still stood, though propped up at one end with bricks. Old, old, why the stove was ancient, thought Esther. Yet it warmed her heart to see it again. Her arm moved as if she were reaching for the handle of her stewpot which used to hang near the stove. The two iron kettles with their fire boxes in the floor had been removed, probably sold for scrap. The smell of fresh onions and garlic filled the air.

"Garlic," said Esther. She smiled at the older Polish woman, who was clasping her hands over her bosom as if too frightened to speak. "My husband, Gerhard, always liked fresh garlic with his beef."

Then Esther noticed that the Polish woman with the dark kerchief wanted to say something to them. In her poverty, the Polish woman understood some of the meaning of this return. Her heart too felt the ache. She too in her youth had been dispossessed when the Red Army broke through into Poland.

She spoke a few words of broken German, remnants of her ancient Catholicism. "Oh, merciful Mother of Mary. Your home, Frau. Your home. Yes, yes, once it was beautiful. Now? Ach." Tears appeared at the corners of her eyes.

When the Claassen clan opened the doors of the van to climb in for the return to Danzig, the dark-clothed peasant woman, tears streaming, beckoned. "Frau, Frau! Wait."

Esther turned from the van door to receive a freshly opened purple iris, jerked from the old bed by the south side of the kitchen. Her iris bed. She had buried the roots there before the war.

"Oh, thank you, thank you." Esther smiled through her tears to the bowing woman. It was like a prayer, the flower that bound them for a moment in both heartache and love. They weren't such strangers after all.

They let Mother Claassen rest longer in her hotel suite when they got back to Danzig. They wouldn't have kept her from the experience, but it had taken its toll. Now they had to fortify themselves.

Tomorrow they would honor Ruth's wishes. "I must go back to Stutthof."

Stutthof Concentration Camp, with its gas chambers and its cremation ovens, was now a museum. Its administration building had decades ago been built by a Mennonite for aged farmers. The Black Spider had changed its destiny.

At 6:30 in the evening, they gathered in the spacious restaurant of the hotel. It was a quiet atmosphere, though the food was too expensive. Nevertheless, nothing can highlight the day for a family like a fine meal together around a table graced with a bouquet of red carnations.

"I believe I'll go to my room." Esther said afterward as she stood, her hazel eyes warmed by the love of family. "If you young folks will excuse me, I'll go to my room. Write a note or two. Maybe take a nap. When do we gather in your room, Ruth, nine o'clock?"

"Nine or thereabouts. A little celebration. Hermann arranged it with *dem Oberkellner* (the head waiter), a little sherry and light dessert, Mother Claassen. Get some rest."

"You boys may be excused." Hermann nodded to the two energetic boys. They had asked permission to stroll along the streets around the hotel and browse among the souvenir shops whose flashing lights invited the tourists.

Sitting at the graceful French Provincial writing desk, Esther wrote a note to her friend back in Düsseldorf, Magdeline Zehr. She signed her name in graceful, disciplined script.

She threw back the quilted spread. *I'll just lie here on my back awhile, rest, pray, ponder the meanings of the day,* she thought. She hadn't really thought about it at all, but it had been taxing. Emotionally taxing.

"Esther. Esther." Half-conscious, she surprised herself. She hadn't intended to go to sleep. Now there was Grandfather Penner again, calling her name.

"Esther, Esther." Others were calling too.

Surprising how the scene took on such a golden glow. Such peaceful light.

She was in Ladekopp church, and Grandfather was at the pulpit, beckoning, "Come, Esther, come."

All of them were there, surrounded by that golden glow. They all turned, smiled, and beckoned, bidding, "Come, Esther, come, come."

Aunt Lottie and Uncle Henry turned around, smiling. "Come, Esther," they said.

It was as if their fall through the terrible ice of the bay were nothing. Nothing at all, no more than someone blowing the fluff from a dandelion head. How sweetly they smiled.

Her eyes glowed. Why, little Hansa! He danced, chubby face spread in a happy smile, little boat in fat hands. "Come on, Mother, come."

And Dr. Rosenbaum from Danzig, wearing his yarmulke. He looked so happy. He stood and beckoned in the light. "My dear Esther, we are waiting for you. Come, Esther."

And this, not even the Danzig synagogue. Surely not a dream. A part of her mind found energy to search its cells. The heart lowered its beat so the golden light could make a full circle.

Why, there was old Beulah Slavanski, and she had

found her rosary. Oh, the joy on her face. And that dark-complexioned man, youngish looking. Gerhard? It *was* Gerhard! My dear husband, I thought he was in the garden picking raspberries.

And Mother Marie and Father Arnold. How sweetly they smiled, not at all worn by the fated trek, the tossing roll of the cold ship. No, it couldn't be."

But it was. They were singing the old song of the Ladekopp Mennonites. Esther Claassen's steps quickened. She surely knew this song. She just couldn't help herself as she slid in the space by that handsome Gerhard. Already, she was singing,

Jesus, still lead on, till our rest be won;
Heav'nly leader, still direct us,
Still support, console, protect us,
Till we safely stand in our fatherland.

Eric Claassen, captivated by the sign above the door, "War Memorabilia," hurried in, eyes widening.

Matthew tried to keep up. Well, he would go in this shop with his cousin, then maybe Eric would take time to spend a few minutes in the bookstore down the block.

The thick, soiled door squeaked. Musty odors met their nostrils. There were old dusty things here.

Eric pushed on in the dim light. Just where was the light anyway? In the back a dim glow seemed to pulse. His arm brushed a suit on a mannequin. Moldy dust drifted down. Sweat broke out on Eric Claassen's neck.

"Uummmmm huhhhhhh, huhhhhhhhh." A low, rumbling laughter coiled in someone's throat.

"Let's get out of here," whispered Matthew.

But Eric was even more energized. "Anyone here?" By now his eyes had grown used to the dimness. He was spellbound by shapes and shadows taking form.

A heavyset man in some kind of uniform rose from a chair behind a counter bearing helmets from ancient wars. Although standing, the figure seemed squat and old. A rancid odor drifted toward the boys. Matthew coughed.

"Two young soldiers, I see. Yes. I admire young soldiers." The figure in the stained uniform leaned over the rubble on the counter toward them. The voice was a cackle.

Then Eric noticed. It was a *woman*. A heavy, old woman in a military uniform, a man's uniform. He clutched at his cousin's arm.

"And what memorabilia do you desire to see, my young soldiers?" She coughed to clear the phlegm from her thick throat. Her rheumy eyes stared at Eric.

"Flaxen hair?" The ancient one crept closer to Matthew, her musty odors engulfing him. "Yes, I see it. Nothing can stop the Aryan blood." She looked over her shoulder as if she realized she had made some mistake. She dared to continue. "Aryan blood, my son." Her laugh reverberated toward the ceiling.

Matthew tugged at his cousin's shirt, whispering, "Let's get out of here. What could we possibly want in this dusty place?"

But Eric's eyes opened wider in response to the dim light and the pull of ancient war medallions, old helmets, bullets, and swords of long-forgotten days. He pawed, he rummaged. He smelled and stroked as his heart quickened and his blood surged.

The old one had seen it before. Many times before. She let him paw through the trifling old memorabilia. Searching, searching. She knew that if she waited the proper inquiry would come.

"Do you have any—" The boy's voice faltered, as if he were about to choke. They always behaved like this.

She waited, tapping her soiled old fingers on the

greasy glass of a counter. When she knew the time was right, she leaned close to his ear and whispered. A question. Only a question. One word. But it hissed. Matthew didn't even hear it. But this sounded like a rudely awakened viper.

Eric turned widened eyes to her cataract-clouded blue ones.

With surprising speed, she waddled to the front door, turning the lock.

Returning to the counter by the boys, she pushed away the bookcase. "This way, my lads. This way. You boys always want what's down in my cellar." Like Eric's, her blood was coursing, her wrinkled cheeks were flushed. "This way, my lads." She lumbered down into the dimness below.

In a far basement corner, a rusty fan manufactured in another era moved the stifling air and fluttered the edge of a huge flag. Dirty red. Old red. As the ancient one closed the door behind her, locking it also, the flag billowed out toward Eric, grazing his forehead. When it furled back in a disgraceful sag, the Black Spider emblazoned on it shuddered and wakened.

Eric Claassen was petrified. Nazi? Oh, God. Black market Nazi memorabilia. His heart pounded. His mind was drunken with anticipation.

"May I ask where you young soldiers are from?" The pale ice eyes were rimmed with the red of old flesh as Olga Fritzenheimer leaned forward through the cobwebs.

She stared ghoulishly at Eric. "And what, my young soldier, is your name?"

Matthew tugged at Eric's arm. But Eric could not be stopped. "Eric. Eric Claassen." He could only whisper hoarsely because of the knocking of his heart. His blood chilled.

"Eric. A name Odin would recognize. Yes. And Claassen. Even though I advanced to the rank of sergeant myself in the Reichswehr (defense force), I once served as a maid in a Claassen home, on what they called the Werder. Yes." The words slid from her wrinkled, warty lips like gas from an unlit burner.

"What do you desire to purchase, my young soldiers of the Aryan race?"

Eric selected an item. The only one he could afford without going to his father. And who would go to their father over this? He wouldn't understand. Even Matthew failed to grasp the significance.

Then Matthew at last dragged from that dingy cavern, tied mysteriously to ancient gods, the reluctant Eric Claassen. Eric, son of Ruth Rosenbaum and Hermann Claassen. The fan whined. The Black Spider awakened more fully.

And Eric gripped the package, filled with something that seemed to him alive and glowing, in his hands. He slipped it inside his shirt. For his wall? For another costume? To wear while reading the new materials coming his way in unmarked envelopes?

"Heil Hitler," hissed the ancient one, daringly, reeking of stale blood and old metal honor badges. "Heil Hitler."

"Heil Hitler." Eric panted, his voice wobbling like a youngster caught in secret pleasures.

And the quickening eggs of the Black Spider stirred on the Hitler Youth armband, the armband like his father and uncle once wore. It lay close to his pounding heart and surging blood.

The Author

Born during the Great Depression of 1929 in Kansas City, Missouri, James D. Yoder spent his early childhood on farms in northern Arkansas and in Garden City, Missouri.

After graduating from Goshen (Ind.) College and Goshen Biblical Seminary, James was drawn by a variety of career interests. He moved from teaching to pastoring, then to teaching and counseling. After receiving a Ph. D. in counseling psychology from the University of Missouri in Kansas City, he became a counseling psychologist and graduate professor at the university. A thread that unified his varied occupations was his belief in the importance of Christian faith and the church.

James was actively involved in the Viktor Frankl Institute of Logotherapy, where he served as diplomate, regional director, and founder of the Institute's Kansas City chapter. This involvement led James to present various papers on logotherapy.

Upon retirement, James and his wife, Lonabelle, moved to the Newton-Hesston area of Kansas. There James has pursued a full-time writing career which has led to such published novels as *The Yoder Outsiders* (Faith &

Life Press, 1988), *Sarah of the Border Wars* (Faith & Life, 1993), and *Barbara: Sarah's Legacy* (Faith & Life, 1994).

The Yoders have one son, Michael. James and Michael are currently working together on a book of meditations. James and Lonabelle are members of the Bethel College Mennonite Church, North Newton, Kansas.